00

POWER OF THE
ZEPHYR

ROWAN OF THE WOOD: BOOK FOUR

POWER OF THE
ZEPHYR

by Christine and Ethan Rose

BLUE
MOOSE
PRESS

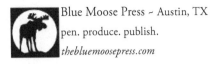

Blue Moose Press ~ Austin, TX
pen. produce. publish.
thebluemoosepress.com

Cover Illustration by J. R. Fleming * http://jrfleming.com/
Edited by Patricia Pneumatikos

ISBN-13: 978-1-936960-94-1
First Edition.

ATTENTION ORGANIZATIONS AND SCHOOLS:
Quantity discounts are available on bulk purchases of this book for educational purposes or fund raising.

For more information and author-signed books, go to
www.christineandethanrose.com * www.rowanofthewood.co

Library of Congress Control Number: 2012915303
Rose, Christine, 1969 -
   Rowan of the Wood / by Christine and Ethan Rose.
1. Wizards—Fiction. I. Rose, Ethan, 1968- II. Title.
ISBN-13: 978-1-936960-94-1

Printed in the United States of America

For Papa & Poppy

CHAPTER ONE

Cullen curled the top right corner of his notebook paper into a tight spiral in one direction, then tried to flatten it again by curling it in the other direction. Doodles filled the margins of the notebook paper, darkening the space above and to the right of the pale pink lines with tight little designs that fit perfectly together, a Tetris of patterns. Forcing his eyes back up to the marker-covered dry erase board, he watched the wild gesturing of his history teacher for a few more moments, but the whispering girls on either side of him distracted him once again. He tried to focus on Mr Grims' lecture, but the task proved impossible.

So much for their summer vacation. Summer school, instead.

Cullen had long ago lost his way in the political maneuverings of post World War II reconstruction which Mr. Grims was taking great pains to explain. Every couple of years he attended a U. S. History class. In a regular semester, the first half of the year got the class through the Revolutionary War. They spent the next week skimming over the War of 1812 and up to the brink of the Civil War. After a couple months slogging through the Civil War, the teacher would make a final dash to cover as much of the last century as he could before the school year ended. He had yet to take a history class that covered the three-year Korean War. All he knew about that was it had lasted through eleven seasons of M*A*S*H. But that was in a normal session. In summer school, everything got rushed together in about six weeks.

The main reason he couldn't concentrate was because his two best friends, April and Maddy, kept whispering excitedly about how much cooler it would be when they were in high school.

"You'll still be going to the same school," Cullen whispered as he studied his ink-stained fingers. In this small town, middle and high school students shared one building.

"Yes." Maddy drew out the one syllable with forced patience. "But we will be high school students. Duh."

"And that will what? Make us popular? Stop Rex and his cronies from picking on us? That is ,if he ever recovers from his temporary insanity as a born-again douchebag. Do you really think things will magically get better for us?"

"No, but we'll practically be adults. Just think about all we could get away with."

"We'll still have the same teachers and have to take the same classes." Cullen motioned to the board with his head. About one quarter of it was separated from the rest of it by a vertical red line. This section was titled "Test Material." Names and dates filled its space. The rest of the board showed a tangle of political connections between a bunch of countries, many of which no longer existed. Mr Grims was illustrating some critical element of negotiations by drawing a line between two of them. When he turned back towards his students, his eyes fell upon the whispering group in the back of the class just as Maddy opened her mouth to respond.

"Maddy, Cullen, April, you might actually benefit from your education if you paid attention."

"I already know all that test stuff." Incorrigible as ever, Maddy answered before those with better sense could stop her. With only one week left until the end of summer school, she felt cocky. This middle-of-the-summer cockiness was surprisingly similar to her beginning-of-the-year cockiness and her end-of-the-year "who cares" attitude.

Mr. Grims clenched his fists, then his jaw. He took a deep breath. And another. On the fourth breath, the maroon of his face started to fade to a rosy hue. The class released their collective breath once they realized Mr. Grims was not going to blow this time. He capped the black dry erase marker in silence and balanced it on its end on the one empty corner of his paper-covered desk. "This," he said with a wave of disgust at the test material on the board, "is not history. It is just a way for students to earn money for their school. It's a glorified bake sale.

"This," he continued with emphasis, pointing to the chaotic diagram of his discussion. "This is real history. The study of history is understanding the way real people, just like us, overcame real difficulties. And how they, in doing so, changed the world that we inherited."

"But we aren't people just like them," argued Maddy, forever pushing it. "They ruled countries and led armies. We're just kids who will probably grow up to work at McDonald's."

"If that is as far as your ambition extends then you probably will. But the rest of us will all participate in the making of history." Mr Grims slipped easily from admonishing back to lecture mode.

"History is a wild ride, a mad stampede of events. It is not created by these central figures. They are just the ones who jump out front and try to guide it. More often than not, they are just reacting to events like the rest of us.

"We study history in an attempt to learn from our mistakes so that we, as a race, do not keep doing the same stupid stuff over and over again. Like basing our national education system after one of the worst state models in the country."

The bell rang at that moment, rescuing the children from further lectures by older and wiser heads that "just didn't get it." This was not Ms. MacFey's Class, so the kids automatically began to climb to their feet and shove books into bags. Ms. MacFey was the only teacher that commanded respect by giving it.

"Geez," Maddy protested as they gathered their stuff. "It's not like we're going to survive high school anyway."

"Count me out of that plan." April crossed her arms in a gesture of determined optimism. She wouldn't let fear and negativity take over. "And careful who you say that to or you'll wind up getting sent to the counselor."

"What are you talking about?" Cullen addressed Maddy, siding with April. Maddy might have a death-wish, but he sure didn't. "Why shouldn't we?"

"Are you kidding? We barely survived the school year, what with vampires and dragons and all. How much longer do you think our luck can last?"

"But everything is okay now." Cullen placed April's cane in her hand and felt her hold onto his hand a little longer than necessary. His face flushed, and he tried to hide it by focusing intently on his feet. Since moving in with Moody, his clothes actually fit him, so he concentrated on the way the hem of his jeans rested perfectly across the tops of his classic Vans.

"Yeah. Right." Maddy let April take her arm and the three of them made their way out of the room.

Cullen stayed just a step behind them. He didn't need Maddy teasing him again. "We did get rid of the dragon, you know. Fiana is gone for good."

"And you still have a sister with a habit of bursting into flame," April teased.

"INORITE?! I mean, things *have* been quiet lately, but I just feel like I'm waiting for the other shoe to drop." Maddy had a tendency to cast doubt on any given situation. In fact, she excelled at it.

"The other shoe has dropped. And we dealt with it."

Cullen wanted so much to believe that everything was going to be okay. Nevertheless, he still had to deal with a magical inhabitant forever occupying his mind. That is, unless Rowan had transformed and was occupying his own body. So Cullen couldn't pretend for very long.

"That's my point. Things keep happening to us. You're not normal, and neither are we anymore. And let's not start with Rowan and Aidan. They're in a different league. We're like an adventure magnet. Sooner or later something is going to slip past our guard and that will be all she wrote."

"All who wrote?"

"I don't know. The fates I guess."

"What is Rowan up to these nights anyway?" April tried to change the subject. It helped to get Maddy on another train of thought before she spiraled down that rabbit hole of despair.

"Just wandering the woods, I guess. We kinda stay out of each other's way as much as possible. All the drug labs have been closed down or moved away, and the growers don't bother him because they don't endanger the trees. I guess there's nothing left for him to do but wander around in the woods."

"He needs a hobby."

"Or a girlfriend." Maddy winked back at Cullen and bit her lip in her mischievous way.

"Ugh! No! He does need something to do, though. I'm a little afraid he'll start going after the loggers."

"Good." Maddy stopped in front of her locker and spun the combination.

"That would be really bad." April leaned on her cane and fixed her eyes as if she looked off into the distance. When she did that, it really seemed as if she was looking at something specific, but without her special gadgets, she could only see blackness.

"If he got arrested would you have to spend your life in prison?" Maddy put her History text on top of the chaos and with some difficulty pulled out her English text.

"That reminds me," said Cullen, ignoring Maddy's question and reaching down into the new backpack his Uncle Marlin had gotten for him. "Do you want to see what the school librarian gave me?"

"Lemme guess. A book?" After checking to see that her makeup was still flawless and her cameo choker centered, Maddy slammed her locker and took April's arm, guiding them to their next stop: April's locker.

"Well, yeah, but it was one they had to pull from the shelves in the late eighties by order of the school board. Since she still can't put it back on the shelf she gave it to me."

"What's it about? Sex?"

Cullen giggled and then blushed. "As if! That's the funny part. It's a kid's book by Dr. Suess."

"What! Like *The Cat in the Hat*?"

"Exactly. It's called *The Lorax*. It's about logging. She told me that so many parents were complaining about their kids coming home and telling them that they were bad for cutting down trees because they read *The Lorax* that the school board voted to remove it from all the school library shelves. She said it's because most of the board members are also mill owners or work for them."

"That's absurd." April opened her locker with a key kept on a pale blue ribbon around her neck.

"Maybe so," continued Cullen, "But she also told me that just before and during World War II, Dr. Suess wrote anti-Nazi propaganda cartoons."

"No way. Only the Nazis used propaganda." April exchanged her History text for the English, stowed it in her bag, and they started for their next class.

"Yeah, way! Apparently everyone was using it then. We just called it something else when we were doing it. Anyway, there is a book of them in the art section. They're not very funny, but they're pretty cool."

"Cartoons aren't art." Maddy seemed very contrary today, which wasn't unusual. She opened the door to Ms. MacFey's classroom just as Josh caught up with them. His standard costume consisted of classic Vans, surfer shorts, and a Hawaiian shirt. When he didn't have anywhere else to be, he could always be found riding the cold waves of the Northern Pacific on his surfboard.

"Hey Cullen, hey April, hey Maddy,"—then in a rush—"you wanna go to the summer dance with me?"

"What, all of us?" cracked April, then busted up laughing. Cullen joined her.

Maddy didn't. "Okay, then, but I'll meet you there."

Everyone was stunned by this reply, even Josh. "Um, really? Okay! Then I'll see you there." He rushed past them into the room in such a state of shock that he sat down in the front row. Josh never sat in the front row. Even though he was in a higher

13

grade, so few kids went to summer school that they were all lumped in one class.

Now it was Maddy's turn to giggle as the three of them made their way to seats in the back row. "There went the biggest foolish grin I have ever seen."

"What are you thinking?" Cullen whispered.

"No one else asked me, and this may be my last chance to go to a dance since I could be dead by the next one."

"Are you hearing this, April?"

"At least she has a date, unlike the rest of us."

"Yeah," said Maddy. "Have you asked Ms. MacFey yet, or has she dumped you for Mr. Ferguson?"

"Very funny. Hey, April, ya wanna go to the dance with me?" Cullen blushed, awed that he had actually had the courage to ask her to the dance. He had practiced time and again in his room in front of the mirror, but it came out way less cool than he had planned. Natch. He held his breath and waited for the laughter, but none came.

Instead, she smiled. She didn't even try to hide her smile, and when April smiled, the entire room lit up. Rays of sunshine filtered in through the dirty window just at that moment, or so it seemed to Cullen. "Well, okay, but only because I can't remember how funny looking you are. Besides, if I don't go, with you we'll both wind up there together anyway."

Images of holding her close as they danced to slow songs filled Cullen's mind, but he knew that the reality of it would probably be quite different. Whereas he was comfortable with April day to day, put in the formal romantic situation of a dance, he was sure he'd be all geeky and awkward. Probably say the wrong thing and ruin everything forever. But, just for now, he dreamed of holding her close and saying all the right things.

The bell rang, jarring him out of his daydream, and just in time to interrupt Maddy's retort. She had already opened her mouth to make some snide comment, but Cullen was saved by that proverbial bell.

It was a good day.

The entire class faced front and became silent. This was Ms. MacFey's class after all.

CHAPTER TWO

Later, in the secret homework lair inside Cullen's new house, the friends sat together studying for the History final. April studied using new technology from Mr. Ferguson, Aidan sat at Moody's desk reading a newspaper for her Current Events assignment, and Cullen quizzed Maddy on past events.

"What was known as 'Seward's Folly?' Was it A, the invitation for Lincoln to join him at Ford's Theater? B, the purchase of Alaska from the Russians? Or C, his endorsement of General Grant for President?"

"Um," replied Maddy as she reached into the cloth bag on her lap. "Just a moment." She pulled out a small twig with a rune carved into it. "Oh, gathering together or collecting. It must be, acquiring Alaska."

Cullen sighed with exaggerated impatience.

"I don't think they're going to let you use April's Ogham when you take the test."

"I got it right, didn't I?"

"Yes, but that's not the point. You're supposed to know the answer without resorting to mystical forces."

"All right, okay, give me another one."

Aidan looked up from her newspaper. "How about what kind of idiot would join a stupid cult called 'The Eternal Cleansing of the Desert Wind'?"

"What the heck is that?" April sat in front of a computer without a monitor, wearing a football helmet almost completely covered with homemade electronics. A brass visor covered her face. The entire monstrosity was plugged into the computer through a USB port. She moved the wireless mouse around in mysterious patterns on a blank sheet of paper clipped into a clipboard on her lap. This was Mr. Ferguson's latest generation of seeing devices for the blind that he was having April test for him.

"According to this article, it is a desert retreat for those in need of a soul colonic." Aidan never put much stock in religious cults or organized dogma of any kind. After her time in the circus, she felt that anyone who followed something blindly deserved what they got.

"Ew-wah!" said Maddy.

"What's a soul colonic?" asked Cullen.

"It's where you go out into the desert and disengage your mind so a special wind can scour your soul while the cult leader drains your bank accounts."

"Hey, maybe that's where Moody is," suggested Maddy.

"Why would he be there?"

"Duh. Questionable sanity. Record of following delusional leaders. You do the math, or rather history. Isn't that why we're studying it, so we can learn from it?"

"Moody wouldn't do that," Aidan protested.

"All right. Okay. I'm just joking. But he has been away for an awfully long time."

"He's trying to get hold of Cullen's legacy," explained Aidan.

"What's taking him so long?"

"The lawyers are insisting that the terms haven't been fulfilled yet, but they won't tell him what exactly those terms are either. And until the terms are fulfilled, the legacy won't be released."

"I'm sure that if it were money the Samuels would have figured out how to get their hands on it already." Cullen's opinion of the Samuels had not improved with their absence. It would take him quite some time to forgive the abuse he suffered under their care.

"Speaking of the S's, how was your date with the social worker? We all know how you like those older women in authority." Maddy never missed an opportunity to tease Cullen, but he had become so accustomed to it that he let it roll right off. He had learned the hard way that the more he reacted, the more she teased.

"It was all right."

"No suspicion that you aren't actually living with the S's anymore?" Maddy had begun to use letters instead of names to affect a Victorian ambiance. She had even given up her modern Goth apparel in favor of Neo-Victorian, a more traditional Gothic style. Cullen thanked the gods that she had not gone as far as wearing bustles, for her own sake. The kids at school who were prone to hurtful behavior made fun of her, but oddly enough, when they had run into some college kids home for the summer, they thought that same look was the coolest thing ever.

"Not a chance," replied Cullen. "These visits are just so they can see that the kid is still alive with no visible bruises. They chat with us alone for an hour or so to give us the opportunity to tell them if we've been abused."

"Why didn't you tell them that long ago?" Maddy, who lived in progressive freedom with her mother and her mother's girlfriend, could never understand that sometimes it was best just to keep quiet about such matters. Of course, if it was her own secrets she was faced with divulging, then mum was most certainly the word.

"I don't know. Fear of the unknown, I guess. I mean, sure, the Samuels were dreadful, but what was the alternative? Some inner city shelter with multiple bullies and no friends."

Cullen trusted government agencies even less than he did the Samuels. These amorphous entities dictated the foundation that his life was built upon, and that foundation was the Samuels' household. If that was the best they could do, then he did not want to experience their second best option. Thank God for Moody and their new arrangement.

"I see your point," said April, who always empathized with his predicament even though her home situation was near-perfect.

"But still, that's just not right. Silence is the abuser's greatest weapon." Miss Empath, however, fought against her inherent power in favor of stubbornness. Maddy had an uncanny ability to play devil's advocate even when she didn't know what she was talking about.

Cullen still didn't rise to the bait. "Well, it all worked out in the end. I mean, look at me. What more could I ask for?" He indicated the lavish library in which they all sat. His new home with Moody was more than comfortable; it was posh.

"Not being put in mortal danger all the time?" Maddy loved those dark clouds.

"Life has its tradeoffs." Even at twelve years old, April knew life contained pain, misunderstanding, and fear. Since her disability encouraged people to pity her and pity was something she couldn't bear, April made a habit of appearing happier than those around her. She trumped their pity. Not that she denied the dark side; she didn't choose to live there.

Sometimes Cullen thought Maddy, burdened as she was with such darkness inside, resented April's light. But Maddy had come a long way in the past few months. He'd rather her be dark and genuine than deceptively happy. She recognized the danger they all lived with and worried about her friends. They all did.

Cullen, on the other hand, lived in his own fantasy world as an escape from the miserable reality of foster care and lost family. Even though fantasy had come true for him in a big way, now that he had his own home and had reunited with his sister, Aidan, he still had a habit of disregarding reality, perhaps as a defense mechanism. "At least Fiana's out of the picture, and all is quiet on the supernatural front."

"Don't be so sure," warned Maddy. "They thought the same about Jason, and look what happened."

"Who's Jason?" asked April.

Maddy sighed. "Halloween one through seventy-four. You know, the movies?"

"Like I watch movies." April made a wide circular gesture around the brass visor covering her sightless eyes, very similar to the around-the-world-and-back snap, without the snap.

"All right. Okay. My bad—I'm just saying."

"We get your point," said Cullen. "But right now I'm more concerned about finishing summer school and salvaging the last bit of freedom before 8th grade."

"Yeah, like you're gonna have problems," sneered Maddy, "especially in English. You'll ace that and the rest like you always have."

"It's not like my studies have been uninterrupted over the past few months. Remember? You know dragons and witches and vampires?"

"Oh, my!" Maddy covered her mouth with her hands.

"Hey, you two," interrupted April, "we're supposed to be studying, not bickering."

"Yes, ma'am," they replied in unison, followed by a community giggle from all three.

"Hey, Aidan," Cullen stood in the doorway to her bedroom exuding nervousness. The girls had left hours ago, and just he and Aidan remained in the main house. Thao and Mai had already retreated to their cottage out back, and Moody was on a mysterious mission. The silence of the house screamed at Cullen without Moody's bellowing laughter, so he went to talk with his sister, just to break the emptiness.

"Yes?" She stood by the window, looking out over the back garden and forest that stretched out behind their home. Sometimes Cullen wondered if she missed the freedom of living on the road. But he couldn't imagine she wanted to be anywhere else than in a cozy home with a loving family.

"Are you going to the dance?"

"Not likely, why?"

"Well, I kinda asked someone." Despair replaced his embarrassment in the flutter of a fairy's wing. "But I don't know anything about dances or dancing, and I'm kinda afraid of looking stupid."

"What?" Aidan, astonished at the prospect of her little brother in love, abandoned her own thoughts and turned to face him. "Really? Who'd you ask?"

"Um, April."

"Oh. I wouldn't worry about it then." She turned back to the window.

"Why not?" Cullen started to focus on the individual stitches along the toes of his socks, wishing he had never started the conversation. Maybe silence wasn't so bad after all. In the embrace of silence and isolation, that's the best place to be sometimes.

"Well, I mean you guys hang out together all the time."

"Yeah, but this is different."

"Ah, young love, romance and all that." Cullen didn't miss the edge of cynicism in her voice. In moments like these, he was reminded about just how hard Aidan had it before coming to live with Moody. The first time he saw her after the fire that had taken their parents' lives, she had been living in a stone cell on a remote island as Fiana's prisoner.

Cullen's cheeks flushed in anger at the memory of it. Or maybe it was out of embarrassment because she'd said 'love.' Was it love? Surely now. I mean, not at twelve, right? "Well, maybe."

"Well, you're asking the wrong girl. I don't know anything about that kind of stuff."

"Yeah, but you are a girl. What would you expect?"

She considered this in silence for a moment before turning to Cullen once again. "I suppose dressing nice would be a good start."

"She won't notice. She can't see what I'm wearing, remember?"

"Oh, she'll know," Aidan assured him. "In fact, you're taking care over something that she wouldn't seem to know about will make a great impression."

"I don't know."

"Look. You asked for my advice. Are you going to listen or are you going to argue?"

"Sorry. What else?"

"Bring her flowers, something that smells nice. So she can't see, but she can smell and taste and hear and feel. Cater to those other senses. She'll like that."

"Okay. What about dancing? I've never danced before."

"Stick to slow dances. You just put your arms around her and move your feet, preferably to the music. Just try not to step on her toes."

"Thanks!" Cullen's mind filled with images of him holding April close to him during a slow dance, whispering the perfect words in her ears. Then she'd laugh, and it would be the sweetest sound he had ever heard. Not that he hadn't heard her laugh lots of times, but this time it will be that soft giggle in response to his romantic wit. He beamed with excitement and nervous anticipation as he made his way back to his room, and he vowed to himself to practice dancing at least one hour a day until the dance.

Somewhere deep inside his mind, a sleepy wizard awoke.

CHAPTER THREE

Fiana watched from behind a curtained window. Her new army gathered beneath her, which is exactly where they belonged. No longer would she pull the strings from the shadows. It was time to come out into the sun, so to speak. But not until the sun went down.

She addressed James without taking her eyes from the gathering congregation of seekers. "Our recruits gather. Just look at them, hungry to believe anything that will give some validation to their miserable and lonely lives."

"Yes." James sprawled on a sumptuous chair behind her, one leg dangling over an ornately carved arm rest. "They've got issues. Never ceases to amaze me, actually. They're looking for some earthy paradise, thinking they can transform their pathetic souls. Truth is: they're hiding. From their past. Themselves. The world. Pathetic. So they come to this desert wasteland to look for answers."

"They don't come *here*, you fool, they come to me, seeking my divine love because they know, deep down in the darkest part of their shriveled little hearts where they are afraid to look, they are not worthy of love. And they're right. They're not worthy of love, certainly not of the true love that survives centuries of adversity."

She bent over James and put a white hand up to her mouth as if to tell a secret and whispered, "But we won't tell them that part."

Turning back to the window, she continued, "They seek it in religion because they know that only a god could love pathetic losers. Idealism. That's what led them to me. The firm belief that the world must be a better place than it seems. It simply has to be. Or at least should be. They're right about that, too. It should, indeed. But it's not, of course. It is what it is. And this is all there is."

"Turning to a leader to answer what they are too cowardly to even ask. To show them something other than the ugly, meaningless truth of their existence." James smoothed the lapels of his dinner jacket.

"If it's lies they want, they won't be disappointed." Fiana had given up her customary green for a pure white robe, greek-goddess style. She must look the part. Appearances, and all that.

"Perhaps this time they will find the goddess they actually deserve," sneered James, dressed to kill. Quite literally. He was ready to stand at his lady's right side as she addressed the masses.

"Oh they will. They always get what they deserve in the end. Don't we all?"

"Indeed." James rose and moved behind Fiana, sliding his hand around her slender waist and looking over her shoulder at the people below. "Just look at them hugging and building a community below, finding mutual support in their quest for truth."

Together they looked down at the gathering masses, who greeted one another with smiles and laugher and hope in their eyes. Old, young, children. All of them blissfully unaware.

"Look at them, James. How simply delicious."

"Indeed. Oh, my lady, look there!" He pointed to a lovely little girl with white-blonde hair riding atop her father's shoulders.

"There is purity in its purist form. Young. Innocent. I bet her skin is soft, and her blood, succulent."

"You do like them young, don't you?"

"So pure and delicious. Nothing compares. Especially that one. See how her hair catches the dying light? Such a sweet child."

"Enough, James. You need to feed. Soon. Now, back to me."

"Yes. Marvelous you. Look at all these outcasts, all here to serve you. They, who fit in nowhere but with other outcasts waiting eagerly for their savior to appear. All seeking some sort of salvation, divinity."

Fiana laughed. "Seeking the divine is a healthy activity. The diseased soul recognizes the need to cleanse itself of its own festering filth and strives to do so. As long as it continues, it is as healthy as can be. It is the soul that has found 'God' which is a lost cause. No petty mortal can find God or hope to understand God. What they think of as God is only their own mass of writhing jealousies, bigotries, and greed subsuming their soul and posing as God. The god they worship is nothing more than a cancerous ego. Ironic, no? Placing themselves and their beliefs above others. Justifying the horrible things they do to each other because their 'God' mandates it. Spouting 'their' Truth. How absurd. Ridiculous."

"You are most wise, my lady, but shouldn't you be preaching to the crowd that eagerly awaits your words of wisdom?"

She frowned at him and the mockery of his statement. She, who was centuries older than he, knew the ways of man and their foolish beliefs. Through this knowledge, she could manipulate them to her will, without the use of much magic at all. Just the sheer need for some kind of answer would suffice, and James had the audacity to mock her.

"I'm practicing, James. One fool is much like another." She emphasized "fool" as she broke from his embrace, taking a step toward the setting sun. "Although you are more of a challenge since you are alone. Foolishness reflects foolishness and it increases exponentially when ever two or more fools gather together. The crowd out there will be easily bent to my will for that very reason. They will be my zombie army."

"Will you have them march to the coast and seize Rowan?" A slight smile betrayed the teasing nature behind his question, and Fiana tensed further. First, mockery of philosophy; now, of her love.

"No need. My little disciple will take care of that for me."

"Shouldn't that statement be followed by insane laughter?"

Fiana had enough. She whirled around with inhuman speed and threw James against the far wall just by willing it to be so. By the time James had regained focus, he saw Fiana standing across the room with arm outstretched towards him. He grimaced in pain at the iron knife sticking from his chest. That, and a rigid countenance were the only visible signs of her displeasure. Her voice remained calm.

"Do you forget that you, too, are just a lackey? A mere play-thing at my whim?"

All humor vanished from James. "I crave your pardon, my lady. I am not worthy to be in your presence."

"Quite right. Yet I need servants, so I will have to endure you. To make sure you remember your place in the future, why don't you continue to wear my little gift until such time as I need it back?"

James grimaced again. "As you wish, my lady."

During this exchange, the sun had slipped completely behind the Granite Mountains. It was time for the show. She turned towards the French doors leading out to the stone balcony.

"Now for a performance that would turn Dr. Mesmer's flesh green with envy, if he had any flesh left on his rotting bones." Using both arms, she thrust the doors open with a dramatic flourish. She strode forth to address the waiting throng. Her voice boomed out across the sea of waiting faces. "Good evening, my fellow seekers," she began. "Today is the day we all begin a new journey together. And with this community of spiritual seekers, we will rise above the pain and heartache of this life and find true joy. True love. True acceptance and the ultimate truth."

The crowd beneath her roared in support.

"Look at all of you! Fine, upstanding citizens seeking truth. Seeking divinity. Look no further, friends. All that you need is within you, and I will show you the way to peace and freedom. No more will your thoughts or fears plague you. No more will you wonder what it's all about. Together, we will come together as one in mind and spirit."

As she continued, she used her powers of telepathy to send a different message, that of servitude. She wove a subtle spell, one capable of encompassing the entire disparate throng, knitting their will into one. With each passing moment, the people's need to serve her utterly and faithfully grew. Through her they would attain all their desires, and with each passing moment their greatest desire was only to serve her.

Her spell made her their salvation.

Upholding her promise, she took their thoughts. She took their fears. She took their doubts.

She took their free will.

She spoke for nearly an hour, mostly because she enjoyed hearing herself speak, but also because mesmerizing this number of people took awhile. If she faced them a few at a time she could cast a quicker, stronger spell that would bind them immediately. After all, she had done that in preparation of this day, when all she had needed were a dozen slaves to devote their lives towards making a habitable home in this desert where the sun shone too bright and often. Now it was time to raise an army. She used her audible words to hold them and her telepathic ones to bind them. Through this silent treachery she gathered them in by the scores.

When she re-entered her throne room, James sat back on the throne, leg over one side, idly stroking the knife handle with one finger.

"Playing with it will only irritate the wound and cause you more pain."

"Yes, my lady." His hand fell away, and he turned his full attention to her. "You were in rare form tonight, truly a great pleasure to hear."

She smiled at his flattery. He had obviously learned his lesson well. "They have been given the pleasure. Now it is time for the pain. Pain to emphasize my control. Set up a rota of private counseling with the teacher for everyone. I will taste them all and my dominance will be complete. Start with Sara Jenkins. She is an investigative reporter here on pretext. Let's make a true believer of her, shall we?

"And get off my throne! I am queen now. Goddess. Pure salvation. Get to work." She melted into the ruby-cushioned throne, spreading the diaphanous sleeves of her white gown until they spilled over the arm rests in a cascading waterfall of fabric.

The evil in her thin smile and mischievous eyes was more maniacal than any laugh has ever been.

CHAPTER FOUR

Cullen hardly recognized the gymnasium where he and his friends did their best to avoid exercise. Even though it shared the same geographic location along the space/time continuum, it had been transformed as if by magic. Well, at least by streamers and balloons and large awkwardly drawn posters trumpeting the dance. The evening darkness embraced its lit interior, illumination transforming the basketball court into an island of light. The fluorescent lights that usually blazed into every corner had been replaced by only the dimmest mood lighting. Cullen usually dreaded entering the door to this chamber of PE torture, but tonight was different. Just before the double doors stood a table behind which sat the vision that was Ms. MacFey and Stephanie, a high school student he knew only by sight. Stephanie traced the edges of a metal cash box with her finger as if struggling not to open it and run away with its contents. Ms. MacFey had her hands folded in front of a roll of tickets. When she saw Cullen approach, she smiled the most beautiful smile, the one Cullen still believed she reserved for him and only him, although he had begun to notice how her smile became a little bit brighter and her eyes filled with joy when Mr. Ferguson would enter the room. But, for the most part, he just pretended that wasn't the case and basked in the beauty that was she.

"Good evening, Cullen! How is my little knight tonight?"

Cullen blushed. As much as he loved being called her 'little knight,' which was her special nickname for him because of his surname Knight, he felt rather embarrassed when Stephanie scoffed in a rude, derisive manner.

Blood rose to his face.

Happy there wasn't a mirror for him to confirm just how red his face had become, he tried to divert both of the ladies' eyes from him by complimenting the gym.

"Hi. Yeah. Fine. Um...they did a great job decorating. Don't you think?"

They both looked into the gymnasium just as he had hoped.

"I guess," Stephanie said, then began fingering the cash box again, forgetting Cullen.

"They sure did. The new seniors worked hard this afternoon to make it look nice. They're anxious to take on their reign in the fall. This is good practice for homecoming and prom." Ms. MacFey turned her attention back to Cullen. "Just one?" she asked, indicating the roll of tickets before her.

"Yeah." Cullen reached for his burgundy and gold striped Hogwarts wallet. He couldn't believe he had to pay to enter this most dreaded portal, but another lovely lady awaited him on the other side. He handed Ms. MacFey a ten dollar bill.

"Of course," Stephanie coughed.

"My date is already inside." Cullen wasn't about to let another insinuation slide. He did have a date tonight for a change. He looked great, after all. Not the nerdy, poorly dressed kid of earlier this year. How dare she assume otherwise?

"Who do you think these are for?" he said, indicating the bouquet in his hand.

"Oh! A date!" Ms. MacFey's eyes got a little twinkly.

Cullen was quite sorry he had said anything at all. Ms. MacFey's enthusiasm and Stephanie's snide comments just made him more nervous, although the fear that made his tummy squiggle and jump at the thought of dancing with April was different from the nausea he usually felt when entering the gym. Any other day, those overactive butterflies in his belly would be more like an urgent desire to use the restroom.

Maybe Aidan had the right idea. She had stated in no uncertain terms that wild dragons could not drag her to a school dance.

He was beginning to understand why.

"Yeah. No big deal."

A disco ball hung from the ceiling, reflecting dancing points of light around the cavernous gym. Cutout stars and paper streamers did their best to give the vast room a festive atmosphere, but fell just short of success. Not enough people to fill the space. Such is a summer dance. At the far end, confident, socially-gifted students, mostly older ones, congregated around the low stage where a young garage band barely managed to play cover songs.

The shy and socially awkward hung around in smaller groups or sat alone near the door, leaving a gulf between the two social poles. Chairs arranged around the walls, facing the dancers, were occupied by girls in party dresses sitting beside other girls in party dresses hoping someone would ask them to dance. Elsewhere, boys unaccustomedly dressed-up, sat alone or in pairs, wishing they had the courage to ask a girl to dance. Most of the regular couples were on the dance floor already, including Maddy and Josh, who were dancing very close.

April stood alone on the far side of the gym. She wore a simple, elegant, light blue dress, not quite full length. Cullen, who usually felt comfortable and open around her, became shy and awkward as he approached.

"Hi," he muttered, looking down at his feet. "You look nice."

"Thanks," she said. "You probably do, too, I expect."

"I suppose. These are for you." He thrust the flowers towards her, but she didn't budge. Then he remembered himself and lifted one of her hands up to the bouquet. She smiled more broadly, then brought them up to her face, inhaling their scent.

"Jasmine! My favorite! Thanks, Cullen, they smell wonderful!"

He stood beside her, looked around, and wondered what to do next. He looked at the seated students, but didn't see anyone he felt comfortable sitting with, meaning Maddy, who was still on the dance floor with Josh. The band now played an up-tempo pop song. She writhed and flailed her body with happy abandon, unconscious and uncaring of anyone's opinion. Josh, for his part shuffled his feet and turned his body stiffly, almost dancing. Maddy seemed ecstatic; Josh, embarrassed.

On the expanse of open floor, more couples faced one another and moved their bodies in synchronized movements that mostly followed the beat.

Cullen groaned inside his head. *What am I doing here?*

"Just have fun," Rowan responded.

I wasn't talking to you! God! Can't a kid have a private thought anymore?

"Cullen, it's okay. You see her every day. Just be yourself."

Whatever.

"Ask her to dance."

Cullen ignored the last suggestion from the wizard, hoping he'd take the hint to shut up and not make this harder than it already was. He didn't know what to do, but he knew he wasn't ready to dance. "Do you want to grab a seat?"

"Okay."

Cullen steered her towards the biggest gap of empty chairs he could see. "Maddy's already dancing with Josh," he informed her. "You should see her go."

"What do you think of her Steampunk dress?"

"It's cool, I guess. She's got a skirt with something on her butt that looks like a tiny bustle."

"Did she at least leave the goggles at home?"

"Looks like it. Huge feather thing around an octopus in her hair, though."

April laughed at this as the song came to a close. As the DJ merged a slow song onto the back of the last, Maddy saw them and waved, grinning widely. She dragged Josh by the hand over to where they sat.

"Hi, April! Hi, Cullen!"

Josh nodded at them. Maddy collapsed into the chair beside April. "OhMaGod! Did Cullen bring you flowers? How adorable." She reached across April and pinched his cheek.

Cullen slapped her hand away, annoyed, and turned the shade of a ripe strawberry.

"Wow! You look really good tonight!"

"Don't sound quite so surprised." Cullen face flushed.

"There it is! I love how you bite your lip like that when you get all embarrassed."

"Stop it." Cullen's face blazed red now, and he made very sure not to bite his lip this time.

Maddy laughed and turned to Josh. "Well, where's my flowers?"

Josh looked calm and serious. "I brought you a corsage."

"Oh, yeah." She looked down to where a white, tropical bloom had been transplanted onto her white, lace-trimmed blouse before turning back to April. "So, has he danced with you yet or what?"

"We just got here."

"So? If you wait for him to make a move you'll spend the whole dance sitting on your butt. Drag him out there and don't let him step on your feet." She plucked the flowers from April's hand and took her cane. "I'll hold these for you."

Cullen, realizing he had no choice, led April to the extreme outer edge of the handful of dancers. He spent an awkward eternity stepping slowly from side to side with his hands on April's hips and her hands on his shoulders. His mind kept asking him to find out what her waist felt like, or maybe just a little bit further back from the sides of her hips, but then all the blood would leave his brain. He'd close his eyes tight for a minute and try to focus on the love song, then he'd notice her lips curved up in a slight smile. Maybe he could kiss her. After all, they had known each other for so long and got along so well, but that would not be okay. Not here in front of everyone.

Left. Right. Left. Right.

Cullen forced his mind back to the sway of the music for another forever until his mind looped around those romantic thoughts again. When, at long last, he was reprieved by the song's end, they went back to their seats.

"Wow, you guys really tore it up out there." Maddy had two tones tonight: mocking and sarcastic, as opposed to her normal tone of sarcastic mocking. But at least she was smiling for a change. She genuinely looked like she was having a great time. Genuinely happy, at least for the moment.

"I don't understand how that's supposed to be fun." He was not amused.

"It's not," said Maddy. "It's the sad remnant of a primitive mating ritual only used by those too young and stupid to know better."

"My, aren't we cynical this evening?" April said before reaching over to pat Cullen on his knee. A rush of excitement filled Cullen; his entire body buzzed with joy.

"I'm quoting my mother, of course," Maddy said, rolling her eyes.

With laughter, their normal comfort around each other returned. Just friends again, hanging out together. Josh remained on the fringe of their discussion, mostly just listening with occasional brief forays into the conversation. Because of his presence, they avoided any of their usual references to their magical adventures. Mostly, they watched their fellow students and made disparaging comments on their dress and activities.

Every once in a while Maddy jumped up exclaiming "I love this song" and dragged Josh onto the dance floor.

Cullen and April talked about them until they came back.

"She seems really happy tonight," Cullen said. "She can't stop smiling. Even when she's taking her habitual shots at me, she does it with this big stupid grin on her face."

"Must be love," April said. "Must be nice to be in love. I hope I am one day."

"Oh, you will be! A girl as pretty and nice as you? You will have lots of boys after you."

Cullen felt a twinge of jealousy grow in his belly, a green monster poking his head up to look around for competition, but no one was around but him.

"Maybe."

"No doubt."

"What about you?"

Cullen's heart leapt up! "Me?" Was she asking what about him as a boyfriend for her? Could she be? "Um...what about me?"

"Yeah. Any girls you've got your eye on? I think I rather fancy Nick. You know, from Algebra? He's funny and pretty nice to me."

The green monster roared and gobbled up Cullen's glowing heart, stamping out its light. "Nick? Oh." Cullen cleared his throat, forcing the beast back down into his gut. "Sure. He's a good guy. But me, no. Not really."

CHAPTER FIVE

Although it would've benefited him much, Rex didn't go to summer school. Instead, he spent the summer scheming about how to carry out his dark angel's orders. He had the perfect plan, and tonight at the end of July, he would finally get to act. No more waiting around.

Rex stomped through the woods enjoying the sound of twigs breaking under his heavy boots. In his right hand, he grasped his Rod of Righteousness, a thirty-ounce, solid hickory baseball bat. Whenever he saw a target of opportunity, he would strike. Young trees, tall stumps, branches that looked like they could be broken. He was a force of destruction visiting his displeasure upon the world.

Many things pissed him off at the moment. Shortly after summer school ended, his stupid foster brother came for a mandatory visit. Cullen's reappearance at home for the social worker charade topped his list of things that pissed him off. Rex hated Cullen and the vile demon that possessed him. That his mother allowed that evil thing back inside his home made his skin crawl. Made him want to vomit. He knew better than anyone else how dangerous that nasty little creature really was. But he couldn't do anything. Just sit there and scowl. The social worker kept looking over at him with wide eyes, but he didn't budge. And he never smiled. Not even once.

His mother. Another thing that pissed him off. When he had tried to tell her about the evil invading their town, she had pretended to listen at first, but then she interrupted to tell him he had better not mess up the sweet deal she had going with Moody. Then she began talking some nonsense about evil existing in principle, not in reality. Just because you didn't like or understand something, she had said, it didn't make it evil. At this point Rex had stopped listening to her, so he really didn't know what else she said. He'd realized that she did not understand the present danger, so he had stopped paying attention. It was that French guy's influence with all those ridiculous French notions. She listened to *that* guy, but not to her own son? WTF-ever.

Rex bashed another redwood trunk with his Rod of Righteousness. The *thwack* echoed through the forest as a warning to the other trees.

To make matters worse, she had told Reverend Timmons, who then came to the house to "have a little chat" with Rex. As the reverend droned on, every word demonstrated his own lack of understanding and belief in the evil that Rex knew as an immediate threat to their community and their very souls. He blocked the reverend out as well, just nodding and saying "Amen" when it seemed appropriate, but he vowed to prove it to everyone. After that "little chat," Rex no longer felt comfortable praying in a church led by an idiot surrounded by superficial believers. They were just going through the motions, living their pathetic lives. He had once been numbered among them, just putting in his time and saying the words. But that was before his personal experience with the evil invading his town. That was before he had seen the true way.

He had been called forth to fight evil.

He was the one on the front lines in this war against evil.

He was the one whom the Angel visited.

He was the one who would deal with Cullen and all his demonic followers.

His angel had told him how, told him where to find the key, told him what to do.

The signal came the night before in the form of a raven, just as his angel had told him it would. Now the time had come. At last.

He brought his Rod of Righteousness around in a mighty two-handed blow against an offending redwood sapling. It's trunk broke with a satisfying crack, and it folded over at the break until its crown touched the ground.

"That's right! Bow down to the Knight of Righteousness and his mighty Rod! All shall bow down before me," he shouted into the empty forest. "All evil shall be treated as such!"

The sound of his words dissipated as if sucked in by the emptiness.

Rex disliked the forest. He found the vast silence oppressive. Any noise he made was quickly swallowed up by the immense solitude. And the trees were much, much too big. Normal trees should not tower so far above mortal man that their tops disappeared from his vision as they got lost in the sky. Nor should they have trunks bigger around than his bedroom. The overall bigness of the forest made him feel small.

He didn't like feeling small.

His own bigness was what made him who he was.

And their age boggled the mind, especially his mind. He'd heard that the old growth trees that had somehow eluded the loggers so far were older than Jesus Christ, something Rex found quite blasphemous.

Even though he generally traveled along the roads, he had spent enough time tramping through the woods to get where he needed to go without getting lost. He'd spent many hours hunting with his father, stalking deer and rabbits in the surrounding hills. But that all ended when his mother had thrown his father out. Then the evil saturating this community had driven him away completely.

Rex would collect his due for that slight as well.

He was making his way through the woods to the house of his science teacher. He had been told the house would be empty tonight. And good thing, too. It had to be done today, so he could get what she needed to her in time for the truce, whatever that meant. It was important that no one interfere with what must be done tonight. His angel never let him down. He could always rely on her, so he wasn't about to let her down either.

Soon enough he came to the edge of the trees and looked across a small field to an old 1930's era house. It was well maintained for its age. From his vantage, he could see the backdoor, which had been replaced with one of those new airtight ones. All the windows were dual paned. Pretty secure overall. But his angel had told him where the key was. No problem there.

He knew no one would be home, and the old house stood alone as far as he could see—no snooping neighbors. He strutted up to the back porch, his Rod of Righteousness resting on his shoulder. A ceramic frog watched his approach from where it nested among the weeds in the neglected flower bed. He pushed it over with the toe of his boot. Underneath it lay a stainless steel key. The lock turned with a smooth and satisfying click, and he was inside. Just like that. It wasn't really breaking and entering. Just entering, really. But maybe he could take his Rod of Righteousness to a few windows anyway. That would certainly make it breaking.

No, better not.

His instructions were to not arouse any suspicion.

But, boy! Would that be fun!

Books and papers covered every flat surface. Although tempted to rummage and find out Ralph's secrets, he figured that he had better just get what he came for. He gave a quick look around the kitchen, listening to the silent house. Feeling its emptiness. Rex was familiar with that feeling and he didn't need more. He headed down to the cellar, just as his angel had instructed. Something was definitely weird about this Ferguson dude. He probably owned the only house in the county, maybe in all of Northern California, with a basement. Rex flipped on the light and stared around him in astonishment.

Before him lay the lair of a mad scientist.

Electronic equipment of all sorts, mostly common items like computers, video games and even hairdryers, covered the tabletops and shelves with their plastic cases open. Snakes of wires ran out of them and into unrelated devices, or they were covered with attachments that simply did not look like they belonged at all. LED dots shone and blinked from multiple places around the room. Chaos. How was he to find what he needed in all this mess? It would take forever.

He sighed and started searching, poking around and moving from one spot to another. Each would turn out to be as fruitless as the last. He was careful to leave everything as he found it, more or less. The angel's instructions were very clear: upset nothing. Raise no suspicion. But, who could tell if anything was out of place or not in all this mess? Still, he would not let her down.

It took him almost an hour to find what he came for. He looked around the basement before shutting off the light. Everything looked as it had when he entered. More or less.

Chaos. Demented, evil chaos which would soon submit to the the cleansing righteousness that he would bring. They might be having it their way now, but soon, soon all that would change.

He patted the bizarre, modified cell phone tucked safely within his pocket.

CHAPTER SIX

The leather soles of Rowan's sheepskin boots barely left an impression as he moved through the dark forest. These evening walks as Cullen slept gave him the opportunity to reconnect with nature and rejuvenate. He understood his place within the countless life forms that interconnected to form a whole in this mystical place. Through this sharing, this merging with that completeness, he gave of himself and, as a result, became more than he was as an intimate part of this world. He had learned to commune with the essence of life when he was just a wee lad, to ground and center himself, to feel the waves of energy emanating from the surrounding foliage and animals. The breeze spoke wise words, if one knew how to listen. The trees, teachers and friends, stood strong even when humans faltered, providing stability to any who needed it.

As Rowan passed each tree, he laid a hand upon the rough bark and closed his eyes, feeling his power mix with that of the great redwood, and through it, the earth. He breathed in this power, feeling each breath continue to heal his broken heart. For although his dear wife, Fiana, had lost her soul and become an evil thing, his love for her and the pain of his losing her to darkness plagued him still. It had been a mere nine months to accept this strange, new reality.

Here in the forest, the place where Rowan felt most at home in this strange time, he could remember her with joy.

He remembered the sound of her laughter and how her hair shone in the sunlight, how her skin glowed in the moonlight.

He remembered how her voice would become softer when she expressed her love to him.

He remembered that same tenderness in her green eyes, full of love when she looked up at him.

She had been so loving and kind, and those images ravaged his memory day in and day out. He found it impossible to believe she was truly evil. Something of her true essence must remain. Even a tiny spark amid all the inner darkness might be enough. With all his heart and soul he hoped for and wished into existence that tiny spark of light.

Regardless, his reality had been shattered, and with it, his heart. Every night he walked through the forest and focused on healing his heart's wound. His path and Fiana's had been intertwined for most of their lives. They had shared love and joy together. The loss of someone so dear, so significant, is never completely healed.

He touched every tree and breathed in its life, holding on to the love he felt and letting go of the pain. Here, he tried to forgive himself for his tragic mistake of hiding away in his wand like a coward all those years ago. A moment of courage would've changed it all. If he could've faced death like a man, none of this would've happened. But that was the past.

This was his reality now.

With each step and each touch on each tree, he tried to forgive himself and tried to heal.

This new age, his prison, mystified and frightened him. He did not belong here. Fortunately, visiting with the trees, who were even older than he was, soothed him. He felt safe here. Free. They helped him carry on. He didn't really want to carry on and thought the best thing for all concerned was for him to just pass into the Otherworld. Disappear. Fade away. Leaving this one to continue without him, but somehow he'd become trapped here.

In the forest, life could flourish in its myriad varieties and become the infinite beauty that it was meant to be. Only nature had the power to heal him.

But tonight, a note of disharmony hung in the air. Rowan felt it in every step. Although he tried to shake it, he could not, for he felt the faintest touch of something out of place and this disturbed him. It was not Fiana. He sensed that she had not been destroyed by Ariel and would return to the attack as soon as she regained her strength. Then it would be up to him to defeat her. He knew that now. Marlin and the kids would help, of course, but ultimately she was his responsibility. Even though he loved her above all else in the world, he knew he would have to destroy her.

If only because he loved her so much.

Perhaps this was why he could not heal.

She might even be behind the disquiet he felt this evening, but it didn't feel like her, at least not her in the flesh. He would know if she were anywhere in the area. Nevertheless, there was a subtle scent of her on whatever this was. Her essence lingered like an unpleasant memory, just out of focus but always, always, always there. That must be what was upsetting his calm so easily.

One of her minions?

If so, not one that has been with her long. The trace of her was too faint.

He stood before the largest and therefore, oldest tree in his immediate vicinity. Planting his feet before it, with the toes of his boots just touching the base of its majestic trunk, he placed both hands flat against its bark. Feeling his energy merge with the tree's, he imagined roots growing out of the soles of his feet deep into the earth beneath him, twisting and turning and weaving down through the dirt and around the rocks and other roots. He breathed in, drawing power from earth through those roots and from the tree and all it touched through his hands, using the combined power and his expanded spirit to probe the world, seeking this anomaly. A possible danger could not be taken lightly, so he always kept watch for it.

As his focus deepened, his sense of the source grew, so he knew it was close. And there was something in addition to that familiar feeling of Fiana. Something he had run into before. He searched his memory over the past few months, blocking out all thoughts and images of his beloved until he matched the sensation. Tracing back months to when he first came to this strange place, when he had first emerged from Cullen. Yes. Then, living inside Cullen and with the Samuels all that time. There it was. That bully. The one he had turned into a mouse when he and his friends had attacked April. Rowan wondered what he was doing in the forest, and more importantly, why his essence was further poisoned with the taste of Fiana. Although a young boy was no match for a powerful wizard like Rowan, with Fiana in the mix, he pulled out his wand just in case. No point in taking chances.

Even as his wand came into his hand, he felt suddenly alone. The connection broken in an instant. Cut off from the world around him. He looked around, bewildered.

Rex stepped out from behind a tree with a thick wooden club, swinging.

Pain exploded within Rowan's skull. His senses reeled in confusion as he fell, desperately stabbing out with his wand and mumbling incantations as he did so. But he had no power. No magic. Even the physical strength of his own hand failed him as Rex plucked the wand from his numb fingers.

Another blow, then blackness enveloped him.

CHAPTER SEVEN

Rex ran through the night mad with glee.

"I did it! I did it!" he screamed into the quiet forest. "I really did it! My angel will be so proud! Yah!" He smashed his Rod of Righteousness against another sapling, breaking the adolescent tree in half. He had defeated the demon and now his angel would reward him. When he saw her again, he'd offer up the wand, and she would shower him with praise.

The thing just looked like a stupid twisted stick, but he knew its power. Well, to be more accurate, he remembered its power. It had turned him and his friends into mice. Kinda hard to forget that. So he didn't want to handle it too much. Not terribly keen on being a mouse again. Plus, he could feel the evil inside it, and it made him sick. He tucked it next to the device he'd stolen from Mr. Ferguson.

That had worked like a beaut, just like his angel said it would.

The demon had became helpless as soon as he pushed the button. Then Pow! Struck down with the Rod of Righteousness! Vengeance was his.

He would never be the mouse again.

His car waited for him on a fire road he wasn't supposed to drive on, but he didn't care. After all, he wasn't even supposed to be driving at fifteen, but he didn't care.

He was on a divine mission.

After Frank had gotten a job as a long-distance trucker, he had no use for it anymore, so Rex's father had returned it to Rex. It wasn't fair that he took it in the first place. It wasn't Rex's fault that his stupid father lost his stupid job and the company car that had gone with it. And now he was completely gone. Things had gotten too uncomfortable for his father once word of his exploits had traveled around town. Fortuna wasn't all that big after all. He couldn't face anyone without being aware of their judgment and the smirks they hid behind their bland faces. Frank had found life much more bearable outside a town where everyone knew his business. Frank had made some excuse about the money being better, but Rex knew the truth. That's one of the gifts his angel had given him. Truth. Reality, as harsh as it was. He understood why Frank left, and now he would leave this good-for-nothing town, too. He would follow in his father's footsteps, but he wouldn't be a trucker. He would be much more important than that.

He would show everyone. His father. His mother. The kids at school, and the teachers, too. He would show them all that Rex Samuels was important, not crazy. Not "emotionally disturbed," as the school counselor had said. But they were right about one thing. He was special. Better than everyone else.

His angel showed him that truth, too.

She saw him for who he really was. Special. Not Special Ed special, but *really special*.

Now he would leave this dead-end town behind him and head towards where the sun rose and a future of glory. Right now. In fact, he wouldn't even wait until morning. He would see the sun rise over the desert, and then he would see the light of his angel smiling at him in gratitude.

Trudy had given up her vodka after visiting France, now finding it vulgar. She had since developed a taste for red wine, as her French boyfriend, Andre, had taught her while in Paris. Red, always red. And he showed her how to properly hold the glass by the stem and smell the bouquet. She felt more sophisticated drinking wine the proper way than she had ever felt with her vodka martinis. Tonight, however, she didn't feel special or elite or anything other than worried. Good thing she kept an emergency flask of vodka in her purse. Just in case.

She sipped deep burgundy wine while pseudo-celebrities practiced their melodrama on the reality show before her. Although it was her favorite show, she wasn't really paying that much attention tonight. Her mind was on her son and his strange behavior of late. Ever since she had kicked Frank's sorry butt out of the house, Rex just hadn't been himself. No longer the adorable mischievous boy she knew, he was surly and serious. Trudy had heard that divorce can be hard on children, but Rex was not a child. He was a head-strong teenager, athlete, self-confident, popular among peers. Or at least he had been. Trudy could not deny the change in him. He had finally taken to religion, something she had been pushing on him his entire life, but there was something strange about his devotion, as he kept talking about praying to angels rather than the Lord Jesus Christ.

And tonight, Rex hadn't come home yet, so Trudy was getting worried. She had tried to call him about an hour ago, only to hear his phone ringing from his bedroom. Following the sound, she found it forgotten on his dresser.

He's just out with his friends; she had soothed herself with that thought for a moment or two and vowed to start calling his friends if he wasn't home by ten. By half-past nine, she had already rung up the parents of everyone on the football team.

All their kids were home safe. And, no, they had not seen Rex all day. She had also been given the impression that her son was not very popular these days. They all said that none of their kids hung out with him anymore, which just worried her further.

Oh, heavens! It must be this holy roller thing!

A proper love of Jesus was only right, of course, but this seeing angels and getting direct messages from God was just going overboard.

She drained her glass and wondered if she should call the Sheriff. Rex was probably fine, just out having a lark like any normal teenage boy. She wouldn't even be worried if he hadn't forgotten his phone, and if she wasn't so lonely. Home felt empty since she had gotten rid of Frank and Cullen had gone to live with Moody. Not that she missed Cullen or Frank, that lying, cheating jerk, but she missed having someone there, especially since knowing Andre and feeling so beautiful and desired again. But he was halfway around the world, and she longed to be back in Paris and back in his arms. Still, she had responsibilities here with Rex, at least until he graduated in a few years. Perhaps then she would move to France for good.

A commercial came on the TV, and she habitually hit the mute button. The sudden, silent emptiness of the house frightened her, weighed on her. Engulfed her. She had gotten used to being the center of a fairly noisy family. But now all that was left of it was her son, and she didn't know where he was. The community was no longer as safe as it had been, and her anxious mind formulated all sorts of unlikely but terrifying scenarios. The silence of the house and muted TV became deafening. All consuming. Closing in around her.

Without another thought, she unmuted the TV and listened to the long list of speed-read side effects of the advertised antidepressant. The incessant noise began to soothe her troubled mind.

Maybe she should call the Sheriff after all. It would at least give her someone to talk to, but then Rex might get a criminal record. Is that even possible? Could they give Rex a record for running away from home at fifteen? Probably. What with everything computerized these days they probably had everyone's grades documented back to kindergarten.

She poured another glass of wine, closed her eyes, and drifted away to Paris.

CHAPTER EIGHT

Cullen awoke to excruciating pain. Throbbing temples where there were no temples. As if someone tightened a vice around his head without the vice. Or the someone. Or the head. He tried to raise his hand. Yep. No hand. He was not corporeal. Suspended in the darkness of Rowan's mind, Cullen wondered what had happened. It felt as though he had been hit, for he had had enough experience of being beaten up in his time. This was definitely that kind of pain.

Shouting into the empty space, void of even Rowan's thoughts, Cullen tried to get his attention. "Hey, Rowan! What's going on?"

His cries all but echoed against the walls of Rowan's skull. Fear welled up in his stomach, or would have if he had had one at the moment. The fear was there whether the stomach was or not.

Rowan didn't answer. Something was definitely wrong. Even in his sleep he answered. But then, Rowan didn't keep control of their body in his sleep. He was far too courteous for that, having long felt as a squatter, he erred on the side of consideration, only taking control of their body during times of trouble or while Cullen slept. Had something happened while he slept? Certainly nothing Rowan couldn't handle. After all, there wasn't much Rowan couldn't handle. Powerful wizard, and all. Even without the magic, he was rather buff.

"Rowan?"

He whispered prayers that went unanswered. It felt too lonely in here by himself. Trapped. Perhaps he was trapped! What if Rowan died while he had the body? Would that mean Cullen would die, too? Or would he change back? Would just the body die and his consciousness be suspended in time for all eternity? Is this what it was like for Rowan in the wand all that time? Scared and alone where no one could hear him or see him?

"Rowan!" The desperate edge to his voiceless voice betrayed his increasing anxiety.

Nothing.

"Deep breath," he said to himself out of habit, for there were no lungs. He focused on his breath the way Rowan had taught him to control his fear. No mouth. No nothing, just thought. Was it even thought? How could it be thought without a mind? Without a brain?

"Focus, Cullen!" He chided himself. Anger had a stronger feeling than fear, so he would hold on to that anger, even if it was turned inward. "Think! If Rowan isn't answering then he must be asleep. And if he is asleep I should be wearing my own body, not trapped inside Rowan's. Maybe he just forgot; that's all. I'm sure he just forgot to relinquish control. Maybe he hit his head and that's where this pain was coming from. It's my body after all, damn it! I'll just take control. That's right. It's my body!"

He concentrated with all his might and willed the change to happen, demanded control. Pushing against the borderless borders of Rowan's mind, of his mind, of where the two met and coexisted, and yet were separate. Through such concentration, his head throbbed all the more, but Cullen pushed through it.

He pictured his body, scrawny and weak. Tousled hair, imperfect vision. Tree-shaped birthmark. He commanded the change with all the mental strength he could muster.

Nothing happened.

Cullen allowed the tension to ease, dissipate. Then he tried again. He couldn't be trapped here forever. He wouldn't be. He shouldn't be! This was his body!

Exhausted, he started to weep tearless tears. Something really didn't feel right. No, not feel. Something *wasn't* right.

Something was most definitely not right.

They could control the changes now. They'd been able to ever since they had figured out how. Well, except for that time Fiana had taken the wand, but that was at the beginning. Right? I mean, had they learned how to change themselves yet at that time? Everything was rushing together. His memories and his fear converged.

"OMG! Had Rowan lost his wand?" Cullen took deep breathless breaths and forced himself to calm down again. He talked himself down; for he was the only company he had anyway. "He wouldn't let that happen. He'd die first, right? Unless Fiana has it again. And she killed him, and now I'm trapped in limbo forever and ever!"

His breathless breaths turned into gaspless gasps. The thumping of his imagined heartbeat quickened against his intangible chest.

Oh, no! What if Rowan had lost his wand?

"Hey, Rowan, wake up!" he demanded, frantic. "Wake up! Wake up! What happened? Are you okay? Rowan!!" Cullen released all control of his panic and shouted and screamed and stomped feetless feet again and again until...

Was that a groan?

"Rowan?"

That one definitely was.

Relief floated over his troubled thoughts and dampened his panic.

Rowan was alive.

If nothing else, at least he wasn't abandoned in limbo forever and ever. As Rowan continued to regain consciousness, the din of his thoughts flooded into the void, populating it once again with comforting life.

Maybe now he could get some answers.

"Rowan, are you there? I need to know what's going on."

"Cullen?" He heard Rowan's voice outside of their body, but it was faint. Weak and frail, like an old man's.

"Yes, Rowan, I'm here. What happened? Are you okay? You really scared me!"

"Attacked."

Stronger, but still faint. Another groan, then motion. Arms pushed Rowan onto hands and knees. Feeling of pine needles on bare knees. Throbbing again. Hand to head. Groan.

"Rowan?" Cullen panicked. "Rowan? Rowan! I can't take this! ROWAN! Tell me what happened!"

A moment. Must recover some strength first. Rowan now thought to Cullen. He was regaining his wits, and this alone helped Cullen relax. Having gone from complete panic to forcing relaxation, back and forth in such a short amount of time was exhausting in itself. Cullen waited and forced himself not to tap his footless foot in his growing impatience, sharing the waves of dizziness and nausea that swept through them as Rowan maneuvered into a sitting position. A few deep breaths, followed by a minimal flow of magic, eased the pain but still left Rowan feeling weak.

"Rowan? Please! I've been terrified. Please tell me what's happened!"

Rowan stood up and opened his eyes. Cullen saw his beloved forest from behind Rowan's blue eyes. Although everything was a little out of focus, at least it no longer felt like a echo chamber of nothingness in here.

It was Rex. He hit me with a club and took my wand. Then he hit me again. That's all I remember.

"Why didn't you turn his sorry ass into a rat?" demanded Cullen.

I think he used Ralph's device to cut me off from the magic. Remember? The one we used on Fiana. He turned it on before he attacked. That's the only explanation. I didn't even hear him approach, Cullen. I never saw it coming. Didn't even feel his presence until it was too late. Then all at once I felt him, that same feeling from the island (which must have been that device), and just a hint of Fiana.

"How would he know to do that? Use Mr. Ferguson's gadget, I mean."

I don't know. Maybe he's working for Fiana and she told him. Why else would I feel her on him, in him? It's the only explanation. Could she really still be alive?

Cullen felt the hope arise in Rowan's soul, and something between anger and disgust overcame him as he realized that Rowan still loved her, even after all she'd done. After the abuse and torture and murder. After keeping Aidan locked away in a dungeon. After hurting all of his friends. After hurting him! After all the lies. The assault. The betrayal. How dare he still love her! She's supposed to be dead. This was supposed to be over.

"So she's back then," Cullen sneered. He didn't even try to hide his repulsion. Why should he? He didn't ask for any of this, and now he was forced to feel Rowan's love for that sociopathic, soulless monster. For one who cannot love. For one who is as empty and void as a black hole. For one who feeds on the love and hope of good people, sucking them dry until they are as empty a husk as she.

"I guess I knew it would happen. How could it not?"

Icy fear clawed at Cullen's soul attempting to replace the hot rage. So many intense emotions emerging back to back made him nauseous. Anxiety and injury erupted in a gorge of puke.

Rowan leaned over and heaved, vomiting on the forest floor.

"Stop, Cullen. Wait!" Rowan shouted into the forest, trying to regain control. *It will be all right, son. Just focus on my breath and let's regain control. The mixture of your anxiety and the sizable bump on my head is not a good combination at the moment. Let us regain control. Breathe together.*

Rowan wiped his mouth and stood, using the trunk of the massive redwood beside him for balance. *Breathing in,* he thought to Cullen, *we inhale the power of the ages. Breathing out, we are calm.*

Cullen's fear subsided enough after a few breaths, but his anger held on.

"How could you?"

I cannot explain it, dear boy. It's love. It does not happen overnight, and it does not dissipate overnight either. We have been in love for most of my life, and yes, she has done horrible things. Every one of her actions since you released me from that wand have been the actions of a monster. A soulless monster, as you so often like to remind me. She lost her soul, Cullen. She gave it up for me. To find me. Do you understand how that weighs on my conscience?

"Of course." Cullen's anger began to fade when he felt the depth of loss again. Rowan had kept his profound grief hidden from him for so long, Cullen thought he was over her. "Of course, I understand that. No one should ever have to go through what you have. But she is not that woman anymore.

She gave up her soul, and although she did it for you, it was centuries ago, Rowan! Now she is dangerous. Very dangerous. Just look at what she's done? Can't you see?"

I can see. I cannot accept it, and yet I do accept it. All at the same time. I feel her in my heart yet. In my soul. I see the spark of goodness that's left in her. It's faint, no doubt, and it is fading fast, but it is a testament to her strength and goodness that it still survives after all she's had to endure.

"You are a fool in love. All those stories and movies now make sense. If this is what love does, then I don't want it. Ever. She's a murderer, Rowan. A monster who feeds on the blood and souls of good people."

Perhaps I am a fool. But I love her still. Not that I will not kill her to protect you or anyone else she tries to hurt. I thought I did already, remember that? I know what I must do, and that pains me as well, but do it I will. Love or no. Love doesn't die so easily, but neither does responsibility and integrity. She may no longer be good, but she once was, and I hold onto the dying hope that she can be again.

"She. Hurts. Other. People. And she enjoys it. If she's still alive, you can bet she's doing a lot of damage wherever she is. To a lot of people. And if you're right, if Rex is working for her, which makes perfect sense being the impressionable, abusive idiot he is, and she has your wand now, she'll be more danger-ous than ever. We have to get that wand back before he gives it to her."

Agreed, but I am too weak and powerless to confront him alone at the moment. We must gather help. I think I could manage to walk home. Let's get back to the house where we can summon reinforcements.

"Okay. You're in the driver's seat."

CHAPTER NINE

Tires crackled over the loose gravel before crunching to a stop. A small cloud of dust formed around Rex's pointy cowboy boot as it hit the ground of the abandoned gas station. After driving just over twenty miles, his butt had started to feel sore, so he was happy to stand up and stretch if nothing else. He was supposed to meet someone here tonight.

Tonight, his life truly started.

The light above the hoseless gas pumps flickered, a psychedelic strobe on the grey cement below. An old sign, hanging from just one hinge, creaked in the breeze. Broken shards were all that remained of the windows in the small station. Inside, nothing but the rocks that had shattered the glass.

A dark lady leaned against the black limousine, crouched behind the empty building, purring softly to itself. Her arms, crossed over her stomach as if for protection, or maybe just out of boredom, relaxed to her sides as she watched Rex cross the dusty yard. A black chauffeur's hat complimented her form-fitting black catsuit which opened just below the woman's breasts, revealing more than a little cleavage.

Rex felt something stir deep in his gut. He hung his thumbs along the inside of the large belt buckle, allowing his hands to hang beneath his protruding belly, and sidled up to the woman doing his best impression of someone important. She most certainly was.

When inferior, act superior.

With a snort and then a spit, he growled, "Who are you?"

"A servant of the angel. Same as you." Her look was that of condescending contempt, but Rex paid that no mind. He wasn't exactly looking at her eyes anymore anyway. "I'm to take you to her temple where you will be honored. That is, of course, if you've completed your task."

"Oh, yeah. I got what she wanted. I got what you want, too."

"Let me see it." She pulled her mouth into a cynical smile, looking him up and down.

Rex missed the mockery in her eyes, as he was too focused on the third button that couldn't stretch far enough to reach its respective hole, just like the two others above it, revealing her milky skin and the fullness of her hidden just beneath the jumpsuit. He let his hands drop a little lower so as not to give away his appreciation of this lovely view.

She reached out and touched his chin, lifting his head until his eyes met the coldness of her own. A mixture of naughty thoughts and an uneasy feeling crept through Rex's stomach, up his spine, and settled into a heavy feeling behind his eyes, filling the emptiness that was normally there. He didn't know whether to kiss her, hit her, or run from her. His Rod of Righteousness was in the car, so hitting her was out. Even for a young man his size, who could easily take this woman, he found her strangely intimidating. And she'd likely hit him if he tried to kiss her, but, boy, she was delicious.

He swallowed hard.

Still, this was not about his fear or his desires.

This was bigger than all that.

This was a fight of good over evil, so he must remain focused. But she was so beautiful. And there she was, so close. He puckered up and leaned in.

She burst out in laughter. "Really?" she said. "Give me the wand, kid."

Rex stepped back, but he didn't look away in embarrassment, no. It wasn't shame he felt at her scoffing; it was contempt. How dare she?

"I'm no kid," he said through clenched teeth and pulled the wand out from the back of his jeans, strange knotty piece of wood that it was. Such a big deal over a stupid stick, but he knew first hand this was no regular stick. He could still remember how he had scurried. Embarrassment followed by anger snuffed out his desire, and the void behind his eyes returned.

"Well done, kid," the driver said as she opened the rear door for him. "Our mistress will be quite pleased. Quite pleased, indeed."

"Wait. I have to get some stuff out of my car."

Rex shuffled back to his car, letting the kid remark slide this time. At least out loud. He kicked up dust with each determined step until he reached his car. "I'll show her who's not a kid. She'll get hers in the end. That's right." After grabbing his Rod of Righteousness and a duffle bag of clothes, he locked the car and threw the keys into the bushes across the road. Won't be needing those anymore. Not where he's going.

"Nice bat," the driver scoffed.

Rex ignored her. She'll get hers. He threw his stuff inside and then climbed into the plush interior. That's right. She'll get hers. It didn't matter, for he knew he was better than this slut anyway. He was the Angel's chosen one, and that made him better than her and all the other whores like her.

Forgetting about her, his attention turned to the leather seats and a small bar to one side. Sliding along the smooth, soft black cushions, he reached for the decanter of alcohol. What kind it was, he didn't care. Scotch. Vodka. Rum. It all took him to the same blissful end. He poured himself a generous amount and savored the smell for a moment before tasting.

As he sipped his drink, the car pulled away from the station onto the road. He turned around to watch his old beater of a car fade into the distance, along with everything he knew, and he felt glad. Goodbye, stupid mother. Goodbye, deadbeat father. Goodbye, nerdy foster brother who doesn't deserve to live in that fancy house. No. Rex deserved the luxury. He was doing good for the world. The work of God through his beloved angel, and that was why he relaxed back into the comfort of the ride, satisfied.

This was more like it, riding in a limo. No more hand-me-down beaters for him. It was first class all the way from now on. He had already forgotten about her laughing in his face. He was really good at not wanting what he couldn't have. But now, with the angel and her plans, there wouldn't be much he couldn't have. Everything. Just like he deserved. Even this slut driver, if he wanted her. Which he didn't.

She's already missed out on all of this, he thought to himself, flexing his bicep.

Yes. This was the life. And it was all his.

CHAPTER TEN

Ralph dreamed of Max. He always dreamt of her. Just as he reached out to touch the softness of her cheek, her face framed by the crashing waves behind her just at sunset, a giant mosquito buzzed and buzzed and buzzed around their heads. He tried to swat it away, and it screamed a shrill sounding scream and then buzzed again.

Ralph woke to see his iPhone dancing across his nightstand as it vibrated and rang. He bolted up and fumbled for his phone with one hand, frantically pressing every button until it stopped making that horrible racket. That ring tone! He must change that blasted ring tone. The old-school telephone sound was just way too loud, especially in the middle of the night. Perhaps something more soothing, a harp instead.

"Hello?" he said after swiping the unlock bar. One hand held it up to his ear while the other fumbled for his glasses. Ah. The world was becoming clearer now. He ran his fingers through his hair.

"Mr. Ferguson. It's Aidan. Cullen's sister."

"Of course, Aidan. It's very late. Is everything okay?"

"Um. Apparently not. Thao just woke me to tell me that someone has stolen Rowan's wand, and now Cullen is trapped inside. Rowan said Rex used your device."

"That's impossible."

"Well, that's what he said."

"That's just impossible," he repeated, still only half awake. His mind hadn't caught up with this new reality yet. "Hold on." He pulled the white earbuds out of the front pocket of his jeans crumpled on the chair by the window. After untangling them by the light of his phone in his otherwise darkened room, he plugged them in and tried again. "Can you hear me?"

"Yes, Mr. Ferguson. Listen to me. Have you had a break in?"

"What? Cullen's trapped?"

"Yes, as I said. Have you had a break in, Mr. Ferguson?"

"Is Cullen okay? Does Max know?" Ralph backtracked as he realized what she meant when she said Cullen is trapped inside. She meant he was trapped inside Rowan!

"You were the first I called, but someone should tell Ms. MacFey soon. Real soon."

"Agreed. I'll do that. My device he said? That's impossible. What exactly did he say? Rowan, that is. What did Rowan say? Is Cullen okay?"

"Look, Mr. Ferguson, we're all a little freaked out here, and I don't know much more than you do. I'm just starting to rally our troops so we can figure all this out. Are you in? 'Cause I have other people to call. You're going to call Ms. MacFey?"

"Yeah. Let me look in my lab first. I can't imagine it's my device. Is Rowan sure?" Ralph spoke through the mic on his headphones and held his phone out to light his path as he navigated through his living room to the stairs.

"He says it was yours." Aidan sighed rather heavily after she said that. She was annoyed. Or worried. But of course she was. *Don't take it personally, Ralph*, he told himself. *She's not annoyed with you. She's just worried about her brother.*

Ralph flipped on the light switch to his basement lab and frowned as he looked around.

"Oh no."

"What is it?"

"Something is definitely not right."

It almost looked right, like the way it would in a parallel universe, similar yet not the same. Occam's Razor suggested another alternative. He turned back to the stairs and then back to his laboratory space.

No sign of an overt break in, but someone had been touching his stuff. Everything was in its proper place, but like it had been moved and carefully put back. Just a feeling he had. Another half-second and he was across the room where his device should be, and sure enough, it was gone.

"I don't know how this happened."

"So it's gone?"

"It's gone. This is disastrous!" Ralph ran his fingers through his mussed hair, trying to smooth it down. It didn't work. Ralph paced around in circles, thinking. Admonishing himself for not having better security in place. "It's all my fault! Damn it, Ralph! You should've been more careful. Cullen is in danger now, and who knows what Rex will do with the wand! I can't believe I could've been so careless! This is disastrous!" His breath came faster and he noticed his heart beating too hard. He grabbed onto the back of his chair and focused on the texture of the upholstery, the coldness of the metal.

"It is what it is, Mr. Ferguson." The calmness of her voice still held that edge of annoyance. Too many years on the edge of survival had given her the instincts of a feral animal, so she was already in survival mode. No use dwelling on what can't be changed. Ralph knew it, and he tried to take a lesson from this young girl. Go. Act. Do. Having a panic attack won't help anyone. Least of all Cullen. But his brain was already in flight mode.

"Okay," he managed between deep breaths. "What next?"

"Let's get moving. You call Ms. MacFey. I'll call the girls. Moody is chartering a flight back as we speak. Thao has already left to pick him up. Let's all meet here in an hour. Deal?"

"Right. You're right. I'll call Max. Good thinking. One hour. You got it."

Ralph hung up and kept trying to control his breathing. The worst of it was passing now. No use in blaming himself now. That could wait until later. Call Max. That's what he had to do. His trembling hands quick-dialed Max. He had just left her side a few hours earlier. After their date, he had been too tired to go to his lab and work, something he did almost every night. If he hadn't dallied so long with her perhaps he would've noticed something earlier. But he found it hard to leave her side. Even when he knew he'd see her again the next day, he found comfort in her presence. Even if she just sat on the other side of the room working on her own. Watching her move, listening to her conduct business on the phone, the sound of her voice. Yes, comfort there. And dangerous, that. Too attached already. But, not now. No use thinking about that now.

"Hello," her sleepy voice said on the other end of the line.

Comfort. Panic averted. Breathe.

"Max. Something's happened..."

Two minutes later, after grabbing a few things, more than he'd likely need, he headed out the door to pick her up. This was going to be a long night.

Aidan had just sent the last text to April and Maddy when the doorbell rang.

That was quick, she thought as she headed for the front door expecting Mr. Ferguson and Ms. MacFey. But when she looked through the peephole she saw an unfamiliar woman. She didn't look evil. But evil people rarely did look evil on the outside. Normally it was the other way around. Aidan had learned that the hard way. This woman didn't look charming or all that beautiful either. Frazzled, more like. Drunk and frantic maybe, but not evil, and certainly not charming.

Wait.

Wasn't that Cullen's foster mom? What was she doing here, especially at this hour? It must be nearing midnight. This was all they needed. As if Cullen wasn't going through enough right now, he'd have to deal with this heartless witch. Maybe she was evil after all. Cullen had told some awful stories about living there.

Aidan yanked open the door. "What are you doing here?"

Trudy didn't feign any civility. "Who are you?" She planted her hands firmly on her hips and looked hard into the sprite's eyes.

"Who am I? You come to my door in the middle of the night and...whatever. I'm Aidan, Cullen's sister. It's late and we're busy. What do you want?"

"Well! I never! How very rude, young lady! Someone should teach you some manners!"

Aidan rolled her eyes and started to close the door, but Trudy softened.

"No, please. I'm sorry. I mean. I'm right," she said with a wag of her bony finger, "but, anyway. Please. I need to talk to Moody right away. It's my son, Rex. He's missing. I think, well, I'm sure if anyone can, Moody can help me get my son back."

"Your son! You've come here about your stupid son? Do you have any idea the trouble he's caused? Nice job raising him, lady. Why should I let you in?"

The woman looked shocked and scared and hurt. Tears filled her lids and her lower lip began to tremble. She was completely out of what wits she had left, which Aidan figured weren't many after the year she had been through. Losing her husband. Losing Cullen. Having Rex for a son, and just, well, being her. Aidan sighed as pity for this haggard woman came over her. She wasn't that old, after all, just thirty-something, but she looked easily a decade older. Deep crow's feet crinkled around eyes black with thick mascara. Tiny black dots punctuated her lower lids. Aidan knew raccoon territory wasn't far behind if Trudy started to cry. "I guess you'd better come in. Moody will be back soonish."

When Trudy, shaken by her encounter with this fierce apparition and sick with worry, crossed the threshold into the opulent home, her eyes went wide with wonder. This was even more beautiful than her dream house. This wasn't just a house; this was a castle! Fine wood everywhere she looked, stained deep and dark and so very rich. Tapestries and paintings and sculptures. Maybe Moody was looking for a companion.

Aidan led her to a large sitting room and showed her to a comfortable chair next to a tattooed man with a red beard resting on the couch. Trudy felt as if she had entered some reality TV show. She almost looked around for hidden cameras, but she couldn't take her eyes off the very large red-haired man stretched out sideways on the couch. Half sitting, half lying down. He wore a green tunic-thingy that looked somewhat the worse for wear and in need of a good wash. The same could be said about the man, actually. His monstrous hand rested on his head as if he had a headache or was deep in thought.

Trudy stood in front of the chair, forgetting how to sit down. Her hands were folded together over her heart and she hadn't blinked since entering the house. So she did just that. Blinked hard. Two or three times, but he was still there. Still in a green dress-like robe. Still with hair too long and too red for any decent grown man. And all those tattoos. How revolting. Maybe he was part of a bizarre biker gang. What kind of people did Moody associate with? Riches or no, she couldn't live like this.

"This is Rowan," said Aidan, motioning for Trudy to sit down again. "You may have met."

He did not look at all like the kind of person Trudy would ever have met.

"I don't believe we have. I'm Trudy Samuels." She resorted to her southern manners in her bafflement and offered her hand in greeting.

"I know who you are." Rowan's gaze met hers for the briefest moment, and she felt the anger behind those eyes before he looked away and focused on the grain of the wood paneling behind the couch.

Nonplussed, Trudy turned back to Aidan for some explanation as to what she had done to offend this large, rude man, but Aidan was similarly cold.

"Why are you here again? Where's Rex?" Aidan demanded.

Trudy broke into sobs and sank into the comfy chair. Between the worry and the wine and the rude behavior and the wine and this strange man and the wine, she couldn't hold back any further. "I don't know! I called all the hospitals. Nothing! I called his friends' mothers, and they said their sons didn't hang out with Rex anymore. I just don't understand." She buried her head in her hands for a moment, crumpling her shoulders and rounding her back. It was as if she shrank into the chair, becoming smaller.

No one knew what to say, so they just waited for someone else to speak first.

They didn't have to wait long before Trudy sprang upright in the chair and continued as if she had never stopped. "He always says he's going out with his friends. So where is he going? I didn't know what else to do, so I called the Sheriff. And...and... and," she said between sobs, "And they found his car abandoned outside of town." This made her wail anew. "I...I think someone took him! My sweet boy! I'm so scared something terrible has happened to him!"

"Do you know what he was up to earlier today?" Aidan said, tossing her a box of tissues.

"I don't know. I mean, he's been different lately, like he's going through a lot of changes. He won't talk to me anymore. He normally goes and hangs out with his friends, I guess, although I don't know what friends anymore. That's what he says he does," she repeated. "I think they might have been playing baseball because he took his bat when he left."

Rowan grunted.

Aidan snorted.

Trudy blinked.

The doorbell rang.

"That must be Max and Ralph. I'll be right back."

"Who?" Trudy asked as she mopped up the black pools that had settled into the sunken skin beneath her eyes.

"A couple of teachers who help us fight evil on their off hours," Aidan tossed over her shoulder as she left the room.

"Fight evil?"

"Long story." Aidan said as she disappeared from the room.

"Fight evil?" Trudy repeated to herself. This is what Rex kept saying. Maybe these people do know what's happening with him. Maybe Moody can really help! But this was all so confusing and everyone was being so mean to her. She blotted her eyes with the tissue again, turning the white tissue into a dripping black mess.

A moment later Aidan returned with a man and a woman. Trudy wondered if the man was Ralph or Max and supposed the other couldn't make it. The woman ran right over to where Rowan lay on the couch and took his hand between hers. The man she came in with didn't look terribly happy about this, for he averted his eyes from them as she sat beside Rowan and asked, "Are you all right?"

"I'll live," Rowan said with a slight smile. "Just a bump on the head."

"And Cullen?"

"Safe, but distraught. Understandably so, given the circumstances."

"He's hurt? Is that why he looks so awful?" Trudy said to Aidan, just realizing that Rowan had been injured. Perhaps that's why he's being so rude. "What happened to him?"

"Your son hit him upside the head a few times with a baseball bat; then he robbed him of something very important. Essential to his existence, you might say."

"No. Never. That couldn't have been Rex! He wouldn't do something like that! He's a good boy! He's my sweet angel-boy!"

Aidan scoffed under her breath, "You're delusional."

"On the contrary," said the man who had just entered with the woman now sitting next to Rowan. "That is exactly the kind of boy he is. Earlier this evening he burgled my house and stole a very dangerous prototype."

"I don't believe it," protested Trudy. "Not my Rex. Never. You must be mistaken. Rex would never do that. He's a good, God-fearing boy. He's a Christian, after all."

Rowan clenched his fists and made a sound very close to growling. The woman patted his shoulder and whispered something in his ear which caused the other man to take off his glasses and clean them with a handkerchief he pulled out of his pocket.

"Believe it," the man said. "We are not going to involve the police in this, but we need to find him and get those items back for his own safety as well as our own. In fact, for the safety of all life on this planet."

This was all far too absurd. It had to be some hidden-camera reality show. Now she looked around for the cameras, smoothing her hair back. She must look a fright! Forcing a laugh, she said, "For the safety of all life. My word! Let's not exaggerate, shall we? I don't believe my boy has anything to do with this. This is all some kind of game, isn't it? This is a trick for a prize, like I see on TV, right? Who are you anyway, sir? An actor?"

"Ralph Ferguson. I teach your son math. And this is Max MacFey, my girlfriend." He put a little too much emphasis on the word 'my' with a harsh glance over to Rowan. "She teaches him English. We know him quite well, Mrs. Samuels, and I don't doubt we see a very different side of him than what you see. He is quite capable of theft and assault and, I fear, much, much worse."

"Have you called the girls?" Max asked Aidan, looking up from her ministrations.

"I texted them. They're going to try to sneak out and get here soon. Tricky, that. Still, without them I just feel like we're the second string team. What with Rowan laid out and Cullen trapped inside, we need more than a fire starter and a wizard without his wand."

"What happened to Cullen? What do you mean trapped inside?" Trudy interjected. "Whatever it is it's not my fault. He's that Moody's responsibility now." She dismissed all this with a wave of her hand, already changing her inner dialogue to have ever even entertained the thought of becoming a part of Moody's life and this circus act, riches or no.

"Don't worry about Cullen," Ralph said, putting his glasses back on. "He's quite safe for the moment, although, probably not too happy about it. It's Rex who is headed for danger. Danger to himself and everyone on this planet, and we're not exaggerating, Mrs. Samuels. We need to figure out where he might have gone. And soon."

CHAPTER ELEVEN

The night had drained away all the colors of the day, leaving only the single spectrum of gray behind. Its range from the cold white of the sodium lamps to the deep black of shrouding shadows veiled all promise and hope with a bitter haze. Most of the misty, flirtatious wisps of fog that had lingered though the early evening had dispersed. Darkness, even where there was light.

The small prop plane taxied to a stop beneath a particularly bright floodlight outside the small terminal. The plane's doors opened like the unfolding beak of a giant, hungry bird, ready to devour its prey. Its gaping mouth made an awning of the top door and stairs of the bottom one. Moody's large, round figure descended. Taking a single step at a time, he balanced himself down to the tarmac. Once he reached the asphalt, he waddled toward the lit interior of the building nearby as he stroked the belly of the large tabby cradled in his left arm, purring contentedly.

Before he reached the hanger, he stopped. He felt something familiar. Too familiar. Something inside him had always told him this day would come. And here it was, on the worst possible day, of course, what with Cullen in danger. But of course it would be today. How could it have been any other day?

"My lady?"

A figure with long, flame-red hair stepped out of the shadows. A pure white streak mingled with the fiery curls just off the right side of her face. Down the left: a black one. Black as the empty, cavernous void inside her hollow shell.

Moody turned towards her and showed no sign of surprise, had anyone besides the cat been watching. But no one else saw this exchange. Just two former companions lost in the gray.

"It's time for you to come home," she hissed.

"My lady, that time is past. You banished me, remember? It was your will to discard me on the streets of New York, all those decades ago. I've paid my debt since, and what a huge debt it was, my lady. The suffering I've known, after being cast from your sight! Have you any idea what that feels like? To have the fabric of one's soul torn to shreds? To be devalued and discarded so callously? I loved you, my lady. With everything I was and ever had been, I loved you. Was devoted to you. I would've done anything for you, as I had proven time and again. I would've died for you. Anything for you, but you got bored with me. You renounced my love. Abandoned me. After these too-long years I have recovered at last. That time is long past when you could say anything to make amends. When a single kind word would've saved my meaningless life. But I have found purpose again. On my own. Without you. It was your will, my lady. *Your* will. There is no going back, too much has changed."

"Nonsense. It was my will, and my will shall always be done. You know that all too well. Now, it is my will for you to return home to me. Do not forget, I own you, Moody. Forever."

"I'm my own man now. You no longer have a hold on me."

At this she laughed, the condescending laugh one would give to a child who is acting foolishly or an adult who has just said something absurd like 'love never dies.' It was the derisive laugh of cynical experience, of superiority over the stupidity of innocence. It was the laugh of someone who had power and who knew she had power and who enjoyed using that power to destroy and to control and to hurt.

She laughed, and Moody felt it in the depths of his round belly. That mocking laugh cracked his soul once again. The very soul he had worked so hard to mend.

She laughed.

"On the contrary," she said. "You gave me the Oath of Oberon. Remember? The Oath of Oberon cannot be broken among those like us, Moody. You know it all too well. If you break the Oath of Oberon, you will lose more than I have ever lost or taken from you. I invoke this sacred oath now."

Moody bowed his head, knowing he had no choice.

"Consider yourself summoned," she spat. She was no longer laughing. Her eyes had turned cold, empty. Frightening. The cruelty and vast emptiness behind them chilled Moody to his very core. "Appear at my court immediately or suffer the correlated doom."

"I understand the strictures, my lady." Moody regained his strength and faced his opponent once again. Standing proud, he met her harrowing gaze with all the warmth and love he could muster, and he could feel every good thing inside him being sucked out. But still, he stood strong, drawing power from the earth beneath his feet. "No need to remind me of that which my people created and hold sacred."

"*Your* people?" Fiana scoffed, curling her lip in disgust. "Your people are dead, Moody. Dust. I am the only family you have left. Come home. Now. I command you."

"On my honor, I have no alternative."

Fiana spun on her spiked heel, throwing her red locks over her shoulder as she strode to her car. She didn't have to look back.

He set the tabby on the ground, and the cat bolted for the protection of the shadows. Moody followed Fiana to her car and, without another word, sank into the backseat. Defeated.

Ms. MacFey set the phone back in its cradle and took a deep breath before turning to the expectant faces. "Well, Moody isn't coming. We're on our own."

"What?" Aidan shouted a little louder than intended, flabbergasted. "What do you mean he isn't coming?"

"Oh, dear," Trudy said.

"I knew it." Maddy was furious and even louder than Aidan. She crossed her arms and plopped down between April and Rowan on the couch. "He went back to *her*, didn't he? I never really trusted him. I told you so, didn't I April? I told her I didn't trust him. Something just doesn't feel right inside him. Never has."

"Don't be ridiculous." April was the only one among them who appeared calm. Even Rowan appeared upset by this news. His brows were furrowed as he looked toward Max to wait for an explanation. April continued, "He wouldn't do that. Look at how good he's been to us and to Cullen. Well, to all of us. He's a good man, Maddy. And you said you didn't trust him, but that was like the week after you said that he was the awesomest guy ever. Remember, when he gave us the runes and stuff? Your *feelings* change a lot. Like, a whole lot. You're still learning how to feel your empathy, and you know it."

"Whatever." Maddy pouted. She wasn't giving in.

"Yeah. Whatever is right." April crossed her arms now, too, and moved as close to the outside arm of the sofa as possible.

Ms. MacFey wrung her hands and bit her lip, waiting for April to finish her defense. "Well, actually, it looks like that might be the case."

"What?" Aidan repeated, this time jumping up from her chair.

"Told you," Maddy said.

"Thao says he met a dark lady when he got off the plane and left with her." Max placed her hand on Ralph's shoulder, and he patted it in support, looking up at her with affection.

"No way!" April sounded adamant. "And even if he did, how can we know it's *her* her? I mean, there are lots of women in the world."

"Why didn't Thao stop him?" Aidan asked the obvious question.

"As if Thao had the power to stop Fiana anyway," Maddy said. "Hello? Have you met her?"

"He hadn't gotten there yet when Moody landed. This is what he heard happened."

"Heard? From who?" Aidan voice held more than a hint of suspicion and frustration at this annoying game of slow reveal. "Just tell us already!"

Ms. MacFey took a deep breath and paused before answering, as if she was trying to find a way to say it just the right way. "Apparently from Sophie."

"Sophie?! Very funny." Aidan said.

"Who's Sophie?" April and Maddy asked in stereo.

"The fluffy tabby Uncle Marlin takes with him everywhere."

"That Sophie?" Maddy's incredulous lilt matched the shocked expression on her face. "A cat?"

"Because nothing weird or impossible ever happens around here. Nothing magical or wondrous or strange. No, nothing at all." April reminded her friends of their reality, backing up Ms.

MacFey and Thao's story. After all, fighting amongst themselves would not help anything. It would only waste more time.

"Good point." Aidan pushed her hair behind her ears and sat down again with a sigh. "Now what? Without Moody, where are we with this plan? I mean, what do we do now?"

"Excuse me," interjected Trudy. "Are you saying a cat told this Thao person that Moody ran off with some woman while my son is missing?"

"Yes. Duh! Keep up." Maddy turned coldly away from her, but April, again, took pity.

"Maddy, don't be mean. Remember how it was when we were first faced with this? It's a lot to take in. Just show some compassion. Feel what it's like to be her right now. Use your gift."

"I'm trying not to feel it. She's screaming in pain and fear, and it's making me nauseous."

"See."

Trudy pushed herself into the back cushion of her chair, trying to melt into it and escape this insanity. "She can feel my... Oh, my. This doesn't make any sense."

"It's a long story, Mrs. Samuels. Let's get you a cup of tea, and we'll catch you up." April stood up and took a few steps towards Trudy's chair. Arm out, she waited.

Trudy looked at the pretty little girl and then around the room at everyone else.

"Um. She's blind, remember? You act like you've never met us before," Maddy said. "You have to guide her into the kitchen. Let her take your elbow."

"Oh. Okay." Trudy stood up and offered April her arm, then led her out of the room.

"You can bring us all some tea," Aidan called after them. "It's going to be a long night."

CHAPTER TWELVE

Fiana's languid figure draped over the high priestess' chair. It was more than a chair, really, especially with her divine figure inhabiting it. Framed in cedar and carved with the stylized animals and knotworks of her Celtic ancestry, it held sumptuous velvet cushions embroidered with similar designs. It was a throne. Her throne. From its plush embrace, she oversaw her cult kingdom, and she smiled. It had been too long coming.

"Honestly, why hadn't I thought of this sooner? I should've done this years ago, James. Just look at them out there, and they're all here to serve me. It is all about me. It is all for me. Me. Me. Me. Me!" She threw her arms up in celebration of herself, then swung her legs over the arm and sat sideways, resting her head on the cushioned armrest and letting her long hair flow freely. It almost touched the floor.

"Indeed." James's tone was dry, almost annoyed. He sat in his own chair, which was far from as opulent and fine as Fiana's, but it was comfortable enough, even with the blasted knife in his sternum.

"My ambitions have been too modest, haven't they? I mean, just a few servants here and there over the centuries. Well, for so long I just had Moody. And what a drag he was most of the time. Glad to be rid of him, at least as my servant, but it's fun to have him back under my control. What a bore. You're much more cheery, James."

"Thank you, madam."

Fiana noticed his tone and spilled off the throne onto the ground, making her way over toward him in a slinky prowl. The bell sleeves created a snowy pool of fabric around her hands with each new step. "Although you weren't very happy that night I found you wailing in the alleyway."

"Yes, my sweet lady. Thank you, again, for the reminder."

"Oh come now, James. It was so long ago. Don't you get all *moody* on me, too." She stopped her playful game and sat before him, leaning back on her hands. "I don't have time for surliness, not anymore. I'd dealt with that long enough with Moody Moody Marlin. Now I want just happiness and joy and bliss all the time. One hundred percent genuine happiness all the time. All day. All night. All the good, and none of the bad. All of the happy, none of the sad. Unless I cause it, of course. But then, making others sad, that makes me happy. Yes, very happy. And they deserve it after all, those peons. What do they know of love and life? They're puppets. If they can be manipulated, they deserve to be, and that makes me happy, watching their pain. Knowing I have the power to cause it. And as long as I'm happy, to hell with everyone else."

Empty-eyed servants, handpicked from her new followers, came in to serve her. They, along with the rest, had been drained of their will and as much blood as they could spare, sometimes a little more if they were particularly fresh and sweet. When she saw them enter, Fiana moved back up to her throne and resumed her queen-like posture. She looked out over her minions again and felt full for the first time in as long as she could remember. The nagging emptiness was filled. Finally. Just as long as she could keep feeding from their veins, and from their souls.

One carried her glass of blood on a silver platter. She raised the chalice and sipped it, dismissing the minion with a lazy wave of her hand. The warm liquid bathed her tongue and lubricated her mouth. She let it linger there, savoring every sensation and flavor before swallowing and repeating her little, decadent ritual again. No more did she devour and rip out throats like an animal. She had risen above.

"I'm quite pleased with my current state of fortune, James. My army of mesmerized zombies increases daily, thanks to my awesome power, which also strengthens daily. It's great how that works. The more servants I make, the more I feed, the more powerful I get, the more servants I make. What a wonderful cycle of joy! For me, at least. Just think of how much more power I will have once I have that wand. And then, once I have my dear husband back in my arms, finally the bliss I've waited lifetimes to experience. So tired of reading about it, of the ecstasy. But only with him. Yes, only with him."

She traced her finger along her collarbone and stared off into the distance, dreaming of what that would be like. Finally. In his arms. Then she jumped suddenly, sloshing the blood over the sides of the glass. The thick red liquid dribbled over her white fingers.

"Curses! James! Call that thing back to clean up this mess!"

"What is it?"

"This stupid phone. It buzzed and scared me. Honestly, this modern world changes faster than even I can keep up with. How do humans do it, being the idiots they are? Remember the age of punch cards, James? That generation is now reaching middle age. Now those punch cards have turned into these little glass bricks. Instant communication of too much information to and from anywhere in the world. From everywhere! It's too much."

"It is rather bizarre, my lady."

With a harrowing shriek, she threw the iPhone across the room, shattering it against the far wall. Then, like a cat, began to lick the blood off her chalky fingers. She caught James watching her, mouth slightly sagging open. "James? The minion?"

"Of course." James moved to the doorway and called down the hall for the servant to return.

Fiana continued her rant, pacing to and fro in front of the balcony, open to the darkened desert below. "Soldiers in fox holes are chatting with their wives on the other side of the world with instant video images. I just don't understand all this nonsense. What's so important? Once upon a time, innovations happened slowly enough that a person could live a lifetime while comfortably keeping pace with the few introduced in their time. It was wondrous and had a kind of magic to it. But now changes happen faster than even mythology can keep up with. Most of today's mythologies are centuries out of date. That's the problem, James. Everyone is disconnected. Mythologies formed to regulate societies that no longer exist have been passed down to descendants who cannot assimilate them into the vastly altered societies they inhabit. As a consequence, many of the young feel a spiritual disconnection. They try to fill this emptiness by seeking new spiritual paths. That's what we're doing here, James! Carving out a new spiritual path!"

She gestured wildly, making grand sweeping motions with her arms indicating the hoards below lit only by the light of the full moon. "A significant portion of these seekers have fallen into my web, and just like other religious leaders who prey upon people desperate to have someone provide the answers to questions they don't even bloody understand, I will do the same for myself. Look, James! Just look at all of them! I *have* done it! I deserve it, after all."

The servant returned with a wet rag and another with a bowl of warm water. As the one wiped her hand clean, the other got down on his hands and knees to clean up the floor around her throne, all while Fiana continued pontificating.

"And they deserve it, too, being the sheep that they are. Weak because of their emotions, their attachments. And I just get stronger. But good for me! Because of their weakness and my growing strength, I reaped a second harvest when family members showed up to rescue their relatives. My power grew as I fed off of their love. Love is such a delicious treat, after all, James! To betray someone using their love. Yes, there's nothing sweeter. And they thought their love was bottomless. Nothing is bottomless, James. Certainly not love. Even though fewer and fewer came, as I mesmerized them all, their *donations* added to my financial resources, increasing with my power! What do they need money for once they're mine? I'm doing them a favor, after all. I'm doing every one of them a favor, James!"

"That you are, my queen."

"My riches grow. My power grows. And even my beauty grows, and I thought that not possible. Look at me! Over fourteen centuries old, and I am as breathtaking as I was on my wedding day. More so, I'd wager. Wouldn't you?"

"Indeed, madam. And what of Moody? What are your plans for him?"

Fiana scoffed. "Moody. What a worthless piece of trash. He's right I discarded him, and good riddance, too. But I need him again now, just to use him, of course, James. To get me to that blasted kid and, thereby, to Rowan. Having him here will draw them to me, just in case the wand isn't enough. And, with him under my power and me with Rowan's wand, they will only have children and that scientist dolt on their side. No match for me."

"Where is he, mum? Moody, I mean. You said you brought him back here?"

"In the dungeons, of course. A special room lined with iron to negate his fey powers. As for my other adversaries, they won't stand a chance once I have that wand in my hands."

She gloated in silent satisfaction at the thought and returned to her throne as the minions scuttled away with their blood-clouded water and dirty rags. They had left a fresh glass of blood for her, and she sipped it, wetting her throat before continuing.

"Rowan is trapped outside that annoying little brat and deprived of his most potent power source as well as his most puissant ally. Yes, indeed, once again everything is going my way and under my control, just as it should be. Just as was before Rowan made his unexpected reappearance. Not that I'm not thrilled to have him back in my life, so to speak. We will be reunited. Soon now, he will be within my power. I'll make the necessary changes to him to allow our inevitable reunion. How else could it end, James? After all this time? And each day my hunger for him grows. It has even surpassed my craving for the stolen blood of life. For the countless souls. Nothing will be enough, James. Nothing will be enough until we are one."

A minion interrupted her reverie by kneeling silently before her throne. For to him, she was a goddess. After all, why not? She was immortal and once had a goddess as a servant, a prisoner. So why couldn't she be a goddess herself? She had the power, and now, the worshipers as well.

Goddess it was.

"I've evolved, James. Do you see that? Don't I look different? I have evolved from mortal, to immortal, to divine. Just look around."

"Yes, my lady. You are indeed a goddess."

She turned and smiled beneficently, if also with a bit of avarice, upon this new minion, still kneeling before her, patiently waiting for her attention. "What word do you bring me?"

"Your worship, the boy you have been waiting for has arrived."

"Ah, excellent. Have him sent in."

The man bowed his head further, nearly touching the tiles, before he got up and retreated.

"James, leave me for a few minutes. We don't want to overwhelm our new guest."

"Of course, mum."

He left, and a beautiful new neophyte soon replaced him (truly, they were unending!). Sara Jenkins, former reporter and current servant, pushed the door open wide to admit Rex.

Fiana was pleased to see that the boy's awe of her had not in the least diminished. Quite the contrary.

Rex gazed about the room, slack-jawed at the sheer opulence of the palace. With wonder and fear written all over his round face, he approached her. Overcome by her glory and his love for her, he just stared not sure what to do next.

She bestowed a smile upon him calculated to increase his adoration of her. It worked perfectly upon his limited intelligence, of course. Such sheep. He was hers unconditionally. She hadn't even needed to mesmerize him. He would follow her because she gave him power over those who frightened him. He would worship her because she had power over him. Just as it should be.

"You have been a good and loyal servant."

"Thank you, my sweet angel." Rex bowed deeply, sweeping his arm in a grand, formal motion because he thought it was expected of him. He'd be right.

"Have you brought me something?"

"Yes, your ladyship. I took the wand just like you said. It's here." He fumbled inside his jacket and pulled out the crooked stick she had sought for so long. He knelt and held it out to her in a reverent posture, like a knight presenting his queen with a magical sword.

She took the wand from his pudgy hands and twisted it between her fingers, feeling Rowan all over it. Once again she held her husband's power in her hands, and no sentimental trick would steal it from her this time. It had been his home for over a thousand years. And now, it was hers. Soon, he would be, too.

"Thank you. You may rise. You have done well and are no doubt tired and hungry after your adventures. Come, sit here at my right and I will have food brought to you." She motioned to a low ottoman beside her throne.

Awkward amid the beauty and elegance of Fiana's court, Rex sat like a troll among faeries. He looked around the room, pleased to be in such fine company, yet nervous because he sensed how out of place he was there.

Fiana could read his thoughts without resorting to magic, and it amused her. It was her knowledge of people, gained over centuries of interaction, that gave her such power over them. Being Moroi and a witch also helped, but her insight was the foundation of her power. She needed no magic to control these weak creatures, but it made it ever so much fun to be able to assault them deeply. Not only their feeble minds, but their bodies and souls as well.

She could read that this dumpy creature beside her suspected that he had never been quite good enough, and he was right. Nor would he ever be. He wasn't as smart as everyone else. His parents didn't have as much money, so his clothes were never as cool or fashionable as the other kids' were. But he was bigger than they were, so he'd compensated with aggression and arrogance. He had learned that he didn't need to be smart when intimidation could get him what he wanted. His emptiness rivaled her own in depth, but he still had that spark of humanity in him, albeit smothered by the fear he kept hidden from everyone, even himself.

A dark haired beauty with empty eyes brought him three sandwiches and a glass of milk.

Fiana watched him devour them. "My! Don't you have a healthy appetite!"

He grunted a reply and continued eating.

She idly played with the wand he had brought her while she watched him eat, fascinated by the speed with which the food disappeared.

When James returned she beckoned him over. "James, this is Rex. He has brought us a stick."

"Ah, excellent." He smiled a cruel smile that should have made Rex nervous if he had been paying attention to James, but Rex was too busy adoring Fiana. James cleared his throat and said, "Welcome to the community."

Rex tried to meet his gaze, but his eyes could not leave what appeared to be a knife handle protruding from the man's chest.

"Um. Dude. Are you okay?"

"James is simply a martyr to our holy cause," Fiana responded, warning James to stay quiet with the briefest flash of her eyes. "I really don't know how I would manage without him. But what am I thinking? Our young guest must be tired." She motioned a minion over, tickled again at how there was always one about. "Escort our young hero to a room where he can wash up and rest from his labors." She turned to Rex and became quite maternal for a moment, feigning concern with perfect precision. "I will speak with you again after you have rested, my dear. Sweet dreams."

She watched him being led away with amusement. This one would be quite entertaining. But in the mean time, there was work to be done. "Is the ritual chamber prepared?"

"Yes, my lady." James bowed to her as he replied. Her demonstration must have been effective. He had become much more polite since acquiring his new adornment. It was a forced politeness that she could taste in the air around her, but no matter. As long as she got her way.

"Well, let's get to work then." She arose from her seat with grace, like the opening of a blossom. James stood and received her proffered hand, then guided her down the three steps of her dais.

"But first, let's pay a brief visit to our other guest."

CHAPTER THIRTEEN

"What has that man done with my son?" Trudy paced back and forth and tugged at her hair, shouting her words as if she blamed the entire world for all her problems. Cullen had witnessed these tirades far too many times and had the good sense to stay quiet and get out of her line of fire.

Maddy didn't.

"Oh, shut up!" she snapped. "Your precious son is the cause of all this mess in the first place."

"What!" Trudy raged, spinning around to face the small, black-haired girl. She put her pointy nose right up to Maddy's and looked into her black-lined eyes with a predator's stare, demanding dominance.

Maddy didn't flinch but rather crossed her arms and strengthened her resolve.

"Well, maybe not the cause, Maddy." Max tried to be fair. "We can only blame Fiana for that, but he is certainly an active, and willing, participant."

When Trudy realized Maddy wouldn't be intimidated, she turned to Max with a bony finger, wagging it in her direction as she stomped and railed: "Now, look here, you overpaid babysitter, Rex is a good boy. I won't hear him spoken of like that by people of your sort."

Trudy quickly learned she was out of her element.

No one here would be bullied because now Max got angry as well and stood up from her seat next to Ralph to face Trudy head-on. "He is not a good boy. He is a bully who derives pleasure from hurting and controlling others, and it's becoming very clear as to where he learned that behavior."

Trudy gasped. "Well! I never!"

"Of that, I'm quite sure, and it's high time," Max quipped.

Reason, as well as tempers, became casualties of the emotional maelstrom brewing within the house. Max and Trudy kept up their shouting match.

Maddy joined in the fun, taking the opportunity to work out her inner frustrations with the situation, her mother, and all condescending adults.

April covered her ears and sat silently within her own darkness.

Rowan put a pillow over his head.

Ralph stared in bewilderment at the combatants.

"Enough!" she Aidan on her feet determined to take charge of the chaos before it drowned them all.

The wood laying in the cold hearth behind her sprang into roaring flame as she spoke. The two candles on the mantle also sprouted flames. Even a few books adjacent to the fireplace caught fire as well.

Stunned into silence, they all stared at Aidan.

"Listen, no more arguing or casting blame. We have taken some losses, reached our darkest hour or whatever, blah blah blah. But if we sit around arguing then we have already lost. It is time to become a team and get the job done. So no more bickering or casting blame." She looked directly at Trudy as she said this. "We'll figure all that out afterward when it doesn't matter anymore."

Rowan peeked out from behind the pillow and put the fiery books out with a wave of his hand.

"I'm not going to give you the Saint Crispin's Day speech, but if you piss me off, crispy is definitely an option. Is everyone cool with that? Because if you're not, the door is over there." Aidan pointed with authority. They all nodded, mutely and in unison.

"Right. Good then. Now what's happened, has happened! Our leadership has been taken from us, so until we get Moody back, I, as the only demonstrably sane person here, am taking charge. Are there any objections?"

April uncovered her ears and smiled.

Maddy plopped down next to her, arms still crossed.

Ralph and Max put their arms around each other.

Trudy looked at her feet and shuffled them about a bit.

Rowan tucked the pillow back under his still-throbbing head.

"Okay, then, let's make some plans. What is our first move?"

Maddy provided an answer. "We need to find out where Fiana is. That's where we'll find the wand, Moody, and Rex. Then we go there, kick her butt *again*, and bring all of them home."

"Okay, good plan. Over to you, Mr. Ferguson. How about doing your mechanical magic and getting a fix on our wicked witch?"

Ralph looked troubled. "I've been trying for months now, just in case she popped up again. I mean, I know we thought she was finished and all back on the island, but I've seen far too many horror movies to know that the end isn't really the end. But, try as I might, I haven't been getting any readings other than Rowan's. At first, I thought she might be really gone, as we thought. But now, that option's out. So she must be masking her signature somehow."

"She must know more about us than we thought," said April. "Somehow she knew enough to send Rex after the muting device. She must have figured out what has been going on and found a way to counteract it."

"Great, now what do we do?" asked Maddy.

"We find another way." Aidan turned to Trudy. "How about you, Mrs. Samuels, can you think of anything Rex might have said that would give us a clue? A starting point? Anything?"

"I don't know." Trudy sat back down in her comfy chair and focused on her hands folded in her lap. "He's been different lately, but it was a good different. You know?" She looked up for signs of support and understanding. "I mean, he just started doing more praying and going to church. He started dressing nicer and always had The Bible with him. He's a good boy. What's wrong with praying? I thought he was growing out of that mischievous stage—he's always been such a little rascal— and really growing up. I have been so proud of him, what with his father and the divorce. I thought he was handling it so well. He was praying! That's always a good thing in anybody."

Maddy rolled her eyes at this pronouncement, but Trudy didn't notice. Her gaze returned to staring at her own hands as if they could somehow help her if they would only do some- thing instead of lying useless in her lap. "I admired his dedica- tion, for I have fallen since the split. Been weak. But I'm only human after all. I never said I was perfect. Rex seemed so pious, and I was proud of him. If I did nothing else right, I raised a good boy."

Maddy snuffed.

Trudy ignored and continued, "But then he started talking about how angels would come visit him and tell him what to do. I started to get a little worried. He'd go on and on about evil taking over our town, about how the forces of darkness were gathering but everyone was either too stupid or too evil themselves to notice. He kept saying that we would all be doomed if it wasn't for him. That I and everyone who wasn't worthy should be worshipping him, thanking him for his service to these angels. Then something about a cleansing wind he would bring to sweep away the evils of the world. You know, that and other crazy-sounding things. Rex always did have a good imagination, so I thought it was just that. Just like his stories about what he'd do to animals when he was younger. I mean, boys will be boys, right? But his stories were so embellished, they just couldn't be true. These were the same. Just exaggerations because he's so imaginative. They just can't be true! But, with all the talk of evil, it rather scared me. So I had Father Tim talk with him, you know, just to set him on the righteous path, but it didn't do much good. Rex stopped talking to me after that. He'd look at me as if I was against him, like I was his enemy. He wouldn't tell me where he went or who he was with. Or, if he did, he'd be vague. Just like *going out with friends—see ya* kinda stuff. I thought he was with his teammates playing sports. But now, I have no idea what he was up to."

"Wait a minute," said April. "That cleansing wind, what does that remind you of?"

"I don't know, what?" Maddy said. "That poem from English class?"

"No, that cult you read about in the paper, you know, the one out in the desert."

"You mean the soul colonic?"

"Yeah, that one."

"Hey, maybe you're on to something," Aidan said. "Good thinking, April! Let's check it out. Maddy, how are your Google skills?"

"Stellar." She moved to the laptop and began navigating while the others kept talking.

Max and Ralph looked at each other in confusion.

April continued questioning Trudy.

"Did your son ever mention what these angels looked like?"

"I think there was just the one who kept coming back. He described her as a tall red-headed beauty surrounded by light. My boy, red-blooded American, he is. Thought it was a fantasy, but he described her in such detail. He said she had a black streak on one side of her hair, and a white one on the other."

"I knew it!" cried April triumphantly. "It had to be her!"

"It had to be who?" Trudy asked, perplexed. "Have you seen this angel, too?"

"Trust me, lady," Aidan said. "This woman is no angel."

Maddy had produced quick results. "Here it is! Check it out. The Eternal Cleansing of the Desert Wind has a website. It not only has an address, but it also has a picture of our old friend James. It looks like he survived the island battle as well and has reinvented himself as a religious leader."

Max turned pale at the mention of his name and raised her hand to the small scars on her neck. Ralph squeezed her hand and gave her a look of love and emotional support, understanding the effects of such trauma take months, if not years, to heal.

"Well then, what are we waiting for? Let's go kick vampire butt!" Aidan had her own trauma to overcome with Fiana. They had all been hurt by her in one way or another, and she wasn't going to take her hurting anyone else sitting down. She stood up, ready to fight.

"The place is in Nevada."

"Oh." Aidan sank back into her chair.

"Vampire?" Trudy said.

"Yeah, 'Oh' is right," Maddy said, ignoring Trudy. "If I survive this trip, I'm going to be grounded for life. There's no way my mother is letting me out of her sight. Not after what happened this Spring."

"I guess just because we know where she is doesn't mean we should just go rushing off after her. We need to come up with a strategy and plan accordingly." Since taking charge, Aidan seemed filled with an increased maturity, despite her knee-jerk reaction to kick some vampire-butt. She took everything more seriously and exhibited little patience for the constant teasing between the younger girls. "So, first things first, we need an excuse to take Maddy and April away for maybe a week."

"I'll work on that," volunteered Max. "I can probably come up with some sort of field trip or something."

"In the middle of the summer?"

"I'll think of something. Extra-credit. Maybe a trip up to Shakespeare's Globe in Oregon! That could work! A special summer road trip for my top students. Paid for by the school, of course."

"Good. Now all we have to do is figure out what we are up against and how to defeat it."

"Or at least rescue Moody, Rex, and Rowan's wand," commented Ralph.

"How is Rowan?" asked Max. "He's been very quiet through this. Maybe he's shut down with all the talk of his wife."

"His wife is a vampire?" Trudy asked.

"He looks like he's sleeping," said Maddy, ignoring Trudy.

"Should he be doing that?" asked Ralph. "He could have a concussion with that blow to the head. Don't forget, Cullen is in there."

"Cullen is in where?" Trudy asked.

"Remember that talk we had over, tea, Mrs. Samuels?" April asked. "Keep up."

"Well, that can't be true. I mean, I thought you were telling me a story to calm me down. You know, some of that fantasy nonsense the kids are into these days."

"Nope. All true."

"But, it can't be."

"Hello. Denial. I really don't have the patience for this," Maddy said.

Max went over to Rowan. "We better wake him up." She shook his shoulder and his eyes opened. "I wasn't sleeping, but I've been focusing all my energy on healing my head. All the arguing made it more painful, so I tuned out and focused inward. I am considerably better and should perhaps join the discussion now. I did hear something about my wife, so I was correct, then? She is still alive?"

"Seems to be."

"I am not sure how I feel about that. Perhaps there is hope for a recovery? You didn't know her before this change. Maybe this is another chance for us to save her."

"Rowan, not as long as she's hurting others. You know this, my dear. She is a monster now. She's not your wife anymore. She has been this way for centuries. I'm afraid there is no going back."

"I don't accept that, but I suppose I must to keep the innocent safe. Well, the innocent and Rex safe. I am considerably better," he said, changing the subject. "Although I am very hungry and should eat soon to help me completely recover my strength."

"Well, that is a relief. So glad you're feeling better. We'll talk more about the rest later, privately. How is Cullen doing? Spirits up?"

"He is annoyed at being trapped inside, but otherwise well. He says hello to everyone, except Trudy. Don't say that aloud. Oh, I see. I misunderstood. My apologies."

April and Maddy laughed.

Trudy looked affronted and bewildered and utterly baffled.

Max blushed, embarrassed for Rowan and for Trudy.

Ralph hid a smile, poorly.

Aidan was all business. "Well, then, all of us who are left are present and accounted for. Let's work on that plan of action."

CHAPTER FOURTEEN

"Mom, can I go to Nevada to help save the world from an evil vampire witch?" April began with the direct approach first thing the next morning. She preferred to be honest whenever she could, something that had become more difficult since Rowan showed up.

"What! No. Vampire witch? What are you talking about?" Joan held the potato peeler in one hand, but dropped the potato on the floor.

"Kidding, gosh!" April picked up the potato as if by sight and handed it back to her mother who started peeling again. "Hash browns this morning?"

"Yep. With real butter. Your favorite!"

"Mmmmm. What else?"

"Pancakes and fakin'bacon."

"Yuk."

"Don't knock it until you try it, sweetie."

"Okay. And I really do want to go on a field trip for extra credit. Can I, pleeeease?"

"In the middle of the summer?"

"It's for Ms. MacFey's class. You know English is my favorite, and she's taking her best students up to Oregon for the Shakespeare Festival at The Globe Theatre! Mom, please? The school is even paying, and it's invitation only. Do you know how special this is to be asked? I brought a permission slip that explains all about it and the itinerary and such."

She handed her mother a blank sheet of paper. Her mother stared at it blankly.

April giggled. "I'm just kidding. I put it on your desk."

"This is the sound of me rolling my eyes. I'll have a look, but you better be nice to your poor old mother if you expect her to sign it."

"Yes ma'am." April knew that to get her way she had to put her mom in a good mood so she didn't trigger any overprotective fears about her blind daughter.

Maddy's mother took considerably more convincing. Even though, after their all-night planning session Ms. MacFey had gotten both girls back home safely before dawn, their mothers none the wiser, suspicion was in the air at the Wells' household.

Aidan, listened as Ms. MacFey talked to Carol over the phone to confirm Maddy's story. Carol was never as trusting as April's mom had been, but especially not after catching Maddy in a lie last Spring and the fallout from that. Maddy didn't talk about it much. They just referred to that time when Maddy was "not well." Still, things were getting better.

"Yes, that's right. No worries, Ms. Wells. She'll be in good hands. There will be two teachers present for every four students." That, at least, wasn't a lie, even if one of those students was trapped inside a wizard. Ms. MacFey looked distressed at having to lie to parents, but it didn't show in her voice.

"That's right. Invitation only! Maddy has really improved this last year, and I think this field trip will give her the confidence and validation to continue. You just need to sign the permission slip and we'll be all set."

The ones we printed out last night on Cullen's computer, Aidan added silently.

"The itinerary is on the website."

The one Ralph created while I was printing the permission forms.

"I understand your concerns, but they will be well chaperoned. Even a parent or guardian, or two, are coming along."

Please don't ask who.

"Why, Trudy Samuels, for one."

Apparently she asked.

After the pause for astonishment and doubt, Ms. MacFey continued, "Yes, Cullen will be going as well, and Rex Samuels, too." Another pause for sheer disbelief.

"Yes, it is invitation for our best students, that's true. But Rex has been trying so hard. And, frankly, he needs the extra credit."

Aidan couldn't listen anymore. It was getting downright painful to hear. So, as the conversation continued, Aidan and Ralph sorted through the supplies they would take with them. Ralph worked from a list which he continually referred to, adding items as he thought of them and checking others off as they were packed.

Aidan's method consisted of running to get anything that occurred to her and picking up any other useful looking items she noticed on the way, then stuffing them in the quickly disappearing nooks in her backpack.

"No, no, there isn't any additional cost, just pocket money for snacks and stuff. The literary club has been raising money all year for this trip." Ms. McFey's patient, authoritative voice did much towards convincing Maddy's mother. It may even have sufficed on its own.

Maddy didn't take that chance. Sitting near the other end of the phone line, she sat looking at her mother with a mild, innocent expression on her face. Inside, where her mother could not see, she focused all her empathic talent towards projecting acceptance upon her mother. She knew she would somehow pay for using her gift to manipulate like this, but it was essential this time. Cullen's and, well, everyone's life was at stake, so it was okay. She normally wouldn't do it, not if it was just so she could go out on a date or to the movies or something. Well, there was that once, but she'd learned. Great power. Responsibility. All that jazz. She projected empathy onto her mother and felt as her mother absorbed it and slowly, gradually softened. That, along with the rational voice of Ms. MacFey, worked a miracle.

The handset went back in its cradle.

"Okay, you can go. But a little more notice next time, Maddy?"

Maddy leapt up grinning and hugged her mom. "I promise, Mom. You know how I forget things. Thanks so much!"

"But no funny stuff."

"No! No funny stuff. I promise! Thanks, Mom. I'll go pack."

Her mother smiled at this unusual display of affection as Maddy ran to her room. Using her empathic abilities to influence her mother's decision really did make her feel guilty. She was betraying the trust of someone who loved her. But what choice did she have? Hello! Saving the world, and all.

The rest of the plan was far sketchier.

After much arguing and persuasion, Trudy had agreed to pose as a convert and infiltrate the Eternal Cleansing of the Desert Wind. She would try to locate Rex and Moody, as well as find Rowan's wand. Once this was done, she would get word to the others who would effect a rescue. How they would manage that they couldn't tell until they knew more. A tall order for someone who had never done this before, but she was in the best position to do so. Fiana hadn't met her, and Trudy had a valid reason to be there: to rescue her son.

Of course, there was Fiana's ability to sense Rowan to contend with as well. That was Mr. Ferguson's department, so they met at Ralph's house for final preparations. Nevada was quite the drive from Fortuna, so they had better get on the road as soon as possible. They didn't have Moody's helicopter or plane to take them this time. And it was best they came in quietly without a big show.

"Welcome to my lair." Ralph gestured at the chaos of electronics and gadgetry around them. Most of them had been there before and knew what to expect, but Trudy kept to herself in a far corner, arms pulled in tight, as if she might catch something terribly contagious just by being in such a place.

"Okay, let's start with some basic communications." He slapped his hands together and rubbed them back and forth, obviously enjoying being in the center of his inventor's domain in front of an appreciative audience. "Maddy, see that cardboard box full of cell phones?"

"This?" Maddy said. "This looks like where cell phones go to die after being tortured with vivisection."

"Um." Ralph gave a nervous laugh. "But they work! Pass those around. Make sure everyone gets one."

Ralph's interest lay in getting things to work. Design elegance came later, if at all, and these "cell phones" hadn't reached that phase. Wires exited the devices randomly and entered a small round box attached to the back. These boxes had been made from the bottom of soda cans. They looked more like a post apocalyptic repair job than cutting edge technology.

Maddy held the box out far from her as each person picked out one of the gadgets.

"Since Moody began helping me fund my research, I've come up with some interesting devices. These are your standard dual-cellphone slash two-way radios, but with enhanced range and capabilities. Moody already has the prototype. Let's hope he still has it on him."

Ralph leaped over to Maddy and picked one out of the box, holding it up with pride.

"The real beauty in modifications is the external antenna. Do you see this extra outlet hole here? Well, you simply plug this end of the adapter in here, and the other end into the ground receptacle of any outlet, and it, in essence, makes an antenna out of the entire electrical system. Even if you were a hundred feet underground, you would get service if you attached this to a ground wire because the signal would travel all the way to the circuit box on the surface. I admit it's probably not something you'll ever use, but in the right situation, it could be very useful. So, be sure you get a phone as well as an adapter and charger."

Bouncing over to the shelves on the far wall, he sifted through a box on the top shelf.

"Now, these are for April, the latest development in magical sight enhancement."

From amidst the electronic clutter, he produced something that had begun life as a set of welding goggles, but had since mutated into a mad scientist's nightmare. Copper and brass dials and forked protrusions surrounded the central lenses. These, themselves, had become telescoping tubes of thin brass with rounded refracted crystal tips. He held them, gazing with awe upon his own creation. "You see these bits here?" He pointed to the protruding copper points. "They act as a sort of antenna, drawing ambient energy into a surrounding field which is focused by their particular pattern into this little gizmo here which will stimulate her, um, mystical talent. These dials here move the two crystals, which form the actual lens, towards or away from each other to achieve optimum optical performance." He beamed with pride at his audience.

"Once more in English," commented Maddy.

"Let's not." Aidan pointed to the time on her lit iPhone. "I assume the straps and buckles are to fasten it around her head?"

"Of course."

"Why not let her strap it on then and she can see how well it works? We've got to get out of here. It's getting late. Nine hour drive, remember?"

Max patted him on his arm. "We are all well aware of your genius dear and are grateful for it. Even if some of us are too rude to show it properly." She glared at Maddy and Aidan.

"She's right, sweetheart. It is getting late. My apologies everyone."

April eagerly tried on the goggles, adjusting them to fit snugly over her eyes with Ralph's assistance.

Rowan caught her arm as she stumbled towards him, then eased her into Ralph's office chair.

"Wow, they're a little disorienting. Can we adjust them more? I don't know what's what."

Ralph helped her fine tune the adjustment, explaining what each knob and thingamabob did.

Rowan kept a steadying hand on her shoulder until she was set.

"Okay, right there. That's better."

She turned her head carefully, looking around the room. "Wow, this is great," she said, standing up, then walking around the room. "They actually work pretty good."

"I think you mean 'well'" corrected Ms. MacFey. That was one of the downsides to going on adventures with your English teacher.

"Of course. I always mean well. It just doesn't always turn out that way." April gave her a mischievous grin.

"I mean, they work well, not good. And that's enough smirking from both of you," she said, pointing to April and Maddy, who had both commenced trying to stifle more snickers. "School may be out, but you'll both be back in my classroom in the Fall."

"Yes, Ms. McFey," chorused the girls, giggling. Max just shook her head and rolled her eyes, smiling at them.

Ralph, a little flustered at having his presentation interrupted by the playful teasing, went over the rest of the gear and ensured everyone had what they needed, as far as they could tell without knowing what to expect.

"Okay. Check list," Ralph said. "Say 'check' to ensure you have the following packed and loaded, if applicable. Holy water super-soakers."

"Check," they all said in more or less unison. Maddy checked on what Rowan had in the backpack Ralph had loaned him, since he was rather lost with the new technology. Trudy didn't say 'check,' but rather made a sound somewhere between a grunt and a whimper.

"Extra holy water."

"Check."

"Stakes and mallets, at least three stakes each."

"Check."

"Cell-phone-two-way-radios, chargers, and adapters."

"Check."

"Flashlight."

"Check."

"Excellent. Now each of you take a cross and hang it around your neck, and there are fresh batteries in that crate on my desk for your flashlights. Make sure you have enough!"

"No, thank you," Rowan said when Maddy offered him a cross.

Trudy scoffed.

"It doesn't work on Fiana anyway, remember? And I'd rather not the reminder."

"Understood, Rowan," Max interjected before Trudy could start preaching. Rowan looked rather pitiful in that torn, dirty robe holding a modern backpack in his large hand. "How's Cullen? He's been really quiet."

"Scared, I think."

"That's understandable, too. We all are," she said, looking deeply into Rowan's eyes directing her reassurance to the small boy trapped within. "Rowan, let's get you out of that robe, shall we?"

Ralph's face turned red and his hands became a little shaky.

"I mean, into something more comfortable. Ralph, can we borrow some jeans and a t-shirt maybe? This robe has had it. And maybe even your shower?"

"So glad someone else said something," Trudy said, and was subsequently ignored.

"Um. Sure. Of course," Ralph said. "I'll take him."

"No. I got this, sweetie. It's fine. I want to talk to Cullen. Start packing, we won't be long."

Max led Rowan up the stairs. "Thank you, Maxine," he said. "I didn't know how to ask. Especially in all the confusion."

"It's okay. I hope I didn't hurt your feelings."

"Not at all."

"So Cullen is okay? Can I talk to him?"

"He has been peeking in and out, but mostly hiding. Well, he says 'No I have not!'"

They both laughed a little at this.

"Now he's angry."

"Oh, sweetie!" Max said, stopping Rowan and looking into his eyes again just after they entered Ralph's bedroom. "We're not laughing at you. We're just all really scared, too. It's okay. It must be hard for you in there."

"He says it is."

"Can I talk to him directly, Rowan? Is that okay?" Her voice softened being so close to Rowan, and she swore he looked as tenderly at her as she felt for him. It was all so complicated with Ralph and Cullen, but she couldn't deny what she felt. Although she couldn't lie to herself, she could choose to act in a way that was right and safe for everyone.

"Of course. I'll just repeat what he says. Does that work?"

"Perfect. How are you, Cullen?"

"I don't like it in here. It's like I'm a ghost in someone else's body, even though I know it's my body. And it's just not fair."

"I know it's not fair, sweetie. I know. This has been so hard on you this past—oh my! Has it been a year? Almost a year. I can't believe it!"

"I can."

Max reminded herself that she was talking to a twelve-year-old boy inside the beautiful man standing before her. His eyes held such compassion and love for, she told herself, the boy. And she felt that love for the boy, too. And for Rowan. And for Ralph. Focus, Max.

"I bet you can. Talk to me. We're about to go on a very long trip."

"So I've heard. I see what's going on around me, Ms. MacFey. I mean, I see it but I'm not of it. Does that make sense? I'm unable to take part, like I'm invisible. Like I don't exist."

"Of course you exist, my sweet." She touched Rowan's cheek and then drew her hand back and looked down at her feet.

"I've been talking, you know. But Rowan hasn't passed on my messages. Like I'm not important enough to be heard—" Rowan spoke for himself again. "That's not the reason, Cullen. You know I was injured, and I've been focusing most my energy on healing. I still have powers, but they are greatly diminished without my wand. It's not that I didn't think it was important, but your words got mixed in with my own thoughts in the pain from the attack."

"I'm sure Rowan didn't mean any harm, Cullen," Ms. MacFey said.

"How do you know?" Rowan spoke for Cullen again. "I mean, what if I'm trapped in here forever? What if Fiana wins? And Trudy hanging around with all of you now just makes it even worse. As for rescuing Rex, well he deserves a stake in his heart as much as Fiana does. The world would only be made a better place by his absence. What if I die in here isolated and alone? Maybe it would be better off without me, too. It hurts not being able to be with my friends or part of their fun teasing ever again. I watch everybody getting ready and planning like it's some TV show I can barely hear. It's like I've been inside here too long now and the real world is a dream. I listen to Maddy and April snicker and joke, and I'm invisible. I don't matter anymore. Everyone has forgotten I even exist!"

"We haven't forgotten, Cullen. We could never forget you."

"I know how you feel, Cullen," Rowan said. "It is how I have felt inside you ever since last Samhain. Forgotten and trapped, but this is our life now. This is our reality now. This is what we have to cope with, whether we like it or not. I swear to you, Cullen, we will find a way to separate us after we're through this. Yes, I know we tried that already, but that doesn't mean we should stop trying. This isn't fair to you, nor is it fair to me."

"We won't stop until we find a way," Max reassured him.

"We promise, Cullen."

Rowan waited for a response, but there was none. "He's gone deep inside, Maxine. I've never felt him like this before, not even when he was hurt and angry. He's gone past pain and frustration and straight into despair and hopelessness."

Max sighed. "Nothing more we can do now, I suppose. We've got to get on the road and get your wand back. Let's get you changed. Ralph's t-shirts might be a bit tight, but thankfully he wears his jeans baggy, so they should fit. The shower is through there. Clean towels in the cupboard," she said pointing to the adjacent bathroom. She handed him a green t-shirt, jeans, and a pair of boxer briefs before turning away. "I'll be downstairs with the others."

CHAPTER FIFTEEN

Moody sat on the floor of his cell, a fat Buddha enjoying the subtle humor of the universe beyond the walls that were, from a certain perspective, temporary illusions. He could see the full moon rising outside the tiny window high above his reach. The moonlight illuminated the iron bars, causing the black metal to shine almost golden. Moody breathed and focused on this sight, blinking only to wet his eyes. He watched as the moon rose higher and higher until he could no longer see it from his vantage point.

A butterfly, pure white, fluttered just outside the window. Strange to see one in the desert. A wind must've carried it far from the vegetation off which it feeds. It was drawn to the brightest light in the area. Amidst the darkness of those in charge here and the muted lights of the mesmerized, Moody's bright inner light shone even brighter, for those that had eyes to see. And this small butterfly did. Attracted to his light, it flew between the bars, did a few loop-de-loops in midair, and landed safely on Moody's outstretched finger. When he saw the frail thing enter, he immediately put his hand up, inviting it over for a safe rest.

"Just you and me in here," he said to the butterfly. "Just you and me. Right now."

The butterfly uncurled its long, thin tongue and then curled it back up again. It twitched its antennae a few times and flapped its wings.

"That's right," Moody said, as if he understood the small thing's language. "But not for long, my dear. No, no. Not for long. And you? You are free to go where you choose. Why are you here?"

The butterfly curled and uncurled, twitched, flapped, and marched its two front legs.

"Ah. Lost. Yes, I figured as much."

A loud thud on the door caused the butterfly to take flight once again, but Moody didn't flinch.

"Safe travels, my friend," he said as it flew back out the window.

"Really?" Fiana said through the small grill in the heavy wooden door. "And I thought I had sealed you off from your creatures. I knew you'd have a kitten here if you could, so I made sure none could get through here. I have *special* plans for any stray that wanders through, as you well remember."

"All too well, my lady." Moody never took his eyes off the moonlit window.

"You seem rather unconcerned at your predicament. Don't you realize that all the power is now in my hands? I will be the one directing events until everything unfolds to my benefit."

"Yes, my lady. Yes, indeed. Everything is, of course, as you say."

"And yet you appear unconcerned, even content. Dare I say peaceful? And we certainly can't have that. I hope you're not expecting your little friends to come for you. There will be no repetition of *that* performance I assure you. I figured out their little energy tricks and have taken the necessary precautions. No, the cavalry will not be riding to your rescue. Well, they may ride, in fact, I'm counting on it, but only to deliver my husband. The rest are expendable. You do know that, right? You do know that plans change, right? You do realize you have no control. No magic. No hope."

"You are quite right my lady, as clever as always. Yes, indeed."

"And yet you do not despair."

"What is the use of despair? As you've so courteously pointed out, I have no control over this situation. If I have no control, I have no choice. If I have no choice, why despair? It would only serve to hurt me. Upset me. Frustrate me. I prefer to live in peace. You are quite right. I have no control. I did what was required of me. I have followed the ancient law and came when summoned. You invoked the geas. Now, events must unfold as they must. They have passed boyond the control of individuals. The universe has taken over. So, yes, I have no control, but neither do you. Don't you see dear lady, the more we try to continue influencing events, the more they will get away from us? Yes, yes, all that's left to do is surrender to the whirlwind and let it take us where it will. And I have surrendered to the universe. Made peace with her. I am at her will now."

"You are at *my* will, Moody! You fool! You always have been! I have set everything up to flow in my direction. It amuses me that you think I'm not in control. You have no idea how much power I have. How much stronger I get every moment."

She held up the twisted, knotty bit of rowan branch that had been the focus of her desire and despair for so long. "And with this little stick, I will acquire control of my wayward husband as well. I will summon him to my will. Then, at last, we will be reunited after all these centuries. Such power will be mine that I will be able to rule the world, if I decide it's worth the trouble. And if you, my dear Moody Marlin, are nice to me, then perhaps I will allow you to serve me again. If you're not, well then, you do not yet know the meaning of the words pain and despair."

With that final word she turned from him and left the dungeon.

Moody listened until her footfalls were so faint he could only hear the distant din of the chanting, mesmerized hordes outside.

"She's gone now," he said.

The butterfly, which had waited on the outer edge of the window away from sight, peeked its head around the opening.

"It's okay," Moody said. "It's safe."

The lovely insect came and sat on Moody's finger. He was happy to have the company. He put his finger up to his nose, and the butterfly climbed onto the bridge. Moody crossed his eyes to focus on the butterfly there and laughed a hearty laugh at the joy of it all.

"You are welcome, my friend."

The butterfly did a little dance on his nose, and Moody responded to it out loud, "She is rather frightening, yes. Dangerous, too. And she's serious about ruling the world, I'm afraid. But she doesn't know something very important. May I share it with you?" Moody dropped his voice to a whisper at these last words.

The butterfly leaped off his nose and flew in two back flips before landing back again.

"I'll take that as an enthusiastic yes! I think I'm very close to finding out exactly what to do that will save Rowan, Cullen, and every one of us. Listen…"

CHAPTER SIXTEEN

With seven people in such a small space for so many hours, their nerves and patience took some damage. Much to Cullen's chagrin, Rowan was in the very back seat of their large, rented van next to Trudy, who tried to convert Rowan to Christianity the entire trip. Her constant chattering fell only on Rowan and Cullen's shared ears, though, as the three girls in the middle seat took refuge in their respective MP3 players. Max and Ralph took turns driving. All their gear was piled up in the space behind Trudy and Rowan.

They left later than they had hoped, so they would unlikely make it there tonight. Their journey began on a long winding road weaving its way through the coastal mountain range. The constant turnings along with the shifting ups and downs got everyone feeling just a little queasy, especially those in the rear seats. Thankfully, Aiden remembered to bring a cooler full of food and snacks from Moody's kitchen, along with some Sprites that settled everyone's stomach through the turns.

The mountains and forests that they drove through possessed a wholesome splendor well worth seeing. However, for the crew in the van, it was the same natural beauty they lived with every day, so the excitement of seeing more of it soon paled, even in the glory of the setting sun. For even the most glorious view, when seen every day, soon becomes merely outside.

"I can't believe we're doing this." Max's thoughts had overflowed her mind and spilt out of her mouth in a low whisper to Ralph. He was taking his turn at the wheel. She didn't want to be overheard by the girls in the back. "They're just kids. What are we thinking, taking them into danger like this? They should be home safe, enjoying their childhood."

"I know. But also understand that they are a part of this. They are probably better able to deal with this than we are."

"Maybe so, but they're still only kids."

"I realize that, but remember that kids have always been the ones thrown into battle to die by their elders." Aidan had been sitting right behind them and had taken out her earbuds to overhear. "I may be young, but I have the blood of an elemental in my veins. I've spent most of my life dealing with this type of thing. I worked through my childhood so I wouldn't starve, and even then I was hungrier than I wanted to be. Kids only a few years older than me are being sent to war zones in Iraq and Afghanistan. Are they children, too? And what about the children over there, even younger than I am, even younger than Maddy and April and Cullen, who are being encouraged to strap bombs onto their bodies and blow themselves up in crowded places as a service to God. For many of us, Ms. MacFey, childhood is a very dangerous time."

"I know, but it shouldn't be that way."

"Maybe someday it won't be, but if that day is going to happen, then we must do what we can today to bring it about. Don't pity us, Ms. MacFey. We have the choice to be here. Many children don't have that choice."

Aidan put her earbuds back and got lost in her music once again.

Max and Ralph sat in silence.

Trudy kept talking.

Grateful to be relieved of the turns, they came down the last pass and onto the long, straight roads of the Central Valley.

And Trudy kept talking.

They drove through the fertile farmlands that brought the first U.S. settlers to this Mexican province, even before the discovery of gold in 1848.

And Trudy kept talking.

Endless fields of cotton and rice flowed past them, orchards and nut groves. Here were the fields that fed and clothed the people of America.

And as the moon rose high above them, Trudy kept talking.

They stopped for gas, a late dinner snack, and to stretch their legs. Within the hour they were once again winding their way through twisted mountain passes, crossing the Sierra Nevadas. The limestone bones of the coastal mountains exposed themselves in the moonlight.

Rowan found the variety of trees fascinating. The diversity far surpossed that of his homeland. On the West coast, the majestic Redwoods towered into the sky with their unique ability to draw moisture in through their leaves. On the eastern slopes, the vegetation tended towards oaks, madrones, in the lower regions, and Douglas firs in the higher elevations. Grasses covered the unforested areas. Slopes were gentle enough to pass as hills.

The Sierra Nevadas presented a more precipitous aspect. Connifers, mostly pines and firs, clung precariously to vertical chasms. Granite showed through in great abundance, interspersed with the foliage. Between the peaks and ridges lay great crevasses through which white waters roiled in a wild dance of life. Rowan watched the glory of nature zip by as Trudy kept talking.

Through this magnificence they drove, mostly silent now, except for Trudy. Road weary and sleepy, they rested as best they could, wanting the trip to be over, but knowing that when it did end, the danger would begin. The girls all dozed after not having slept the night before. Max caught a few winks when Ralph drove, and vice versa. Finally, around midnight, even Trudy drifted off to sleep, resting her head on Rowan's strong shoulder.

Somewhere near the border of Nevada, Ralph pulled into a rest area to catch an hour or two of sleep before continuing on their journey. They wanted to be at the office when it opened at nine, and there were still two hours to Reno, then another two or three after that. But if he didn't get at least a few hours, he'd be jeopardizing all their safety. Better to be safe than road kill. Just an hour or two.

CHAPTER SEVENTEEN

Fiana descended into a secret and secure cavern, far underground where the desert heat did not penetrate. Here it felt cool, even to her cold skin. Cold and dark, just the way she liked it. Here she kept all that was needed to perform the necessary magics, just in case the simple boy and the simpering man weren't enough to lure them.

James waited there for her, knife still sticking out of his chest.

"How is Moody?"

"Humorously optimistic. Or, perhaps, I should say foolishly optimistic."

"I've brought the heart, my lady."

"Very good. The full Lughnasadh moon, James. Perfect for the ritual tonight. How lucky we were that the full moon fell on the eve of Lughnasadh this year!"

"Indeed."

"How silly of me. It's not luck; it's fate! It's the entire universe coming together at this very moment to empower me, just as it should be."

"What of this ritual, my lady? What will it do?"

"Draw Rowan to me. Lughasadh begins the time of truce, powerful first day of August, especially under this gorgeous moon. I'm surging with power! Under the upcoming truce of our peoples, Rowan will walk willingly into my arms, and we will be united. Forever."

"That sounds quite easy, mum."

"Easy?! Have you any idea what I've been through to come to this point? Anything but easy."

"I just meant that—"

"Do shut up, James. Enough of your prattle. I must get to work. Where is the heart?"

"Here."

He opened a wooden box and inside was a small, human heart.

"Virgin?"

"Of course, my goddess. Pure. And very young, not a day over eight years old I would guess. Her blood tasted like copper ice cream." James licked his fingers and remembered.

"And it's fresh?"

"Still warm."

"Oh, James! It is," Fiana said as she took the small thing into her hands. Holding it over a black iron cauldron, she squeezed and wrung the child's heart until not a drop of blood was left. She bit into it, as if eating an apple, and laughed. A single drop of blood oozed from the corner of her mouth, down her chin.

"What is so funny, my lady?"

"Moody was right about one thing. None of my adversaries can do a thing to stop me."

James assisted her through the rest of the ritual as best he could. He lacked the abilities of her former servant, Moody, but she was powerful enough for them both. She mixed other dark fluids with the blood and spoke words of power in a language long forgotten. The fresh scents of the herbs she crushed mingled with the odors of burning incense and the metallic smell of the child's blood. When the entire mixture was complete, she set up the spell. Lit by candles made from the earwax of goblins, she prepared the altar, while James placed bronze braziers in strategic places around the chamber which sprang into flame with a whisper from Fiana's lips. In the center of the altar, she placed Rowan's wand within a large earthenware bowl of sea water. Drop by drop, she dribbled the blood and herb concoction into the seawater, taking great delight to watch the dark, lumpy liquid swirl and pollute the clear seawater.

"As these mingling liquids, light and dark, hold the bonds of my magic, so will Rowan be mingled with me, light and dark, and held within my power. We will be one."

She swirled the air above the mixture with her own magic wand, whispering incantations, until the liquid swirled along with the motion and velocity of her wand. Rising up, she coaxed the muddy concoction out of the bowl. It balanced Rowan's wand on the top of its magical whirlwind as it spun faster and faster. Fiana thrust her arms apart and the tower of watery blood followed, splitting down the middle and staining the stone walls on either side. Rowan's wand fell back into the bowl, unharmed.

She picked up his wand and held it next to her own. With a pure black satin cord, she wound the two wands together, held them close to her breast, and kissed the tip of each.

"So it is finished."

She looked over at James, who was stained with the foul mixture.

"Nice work, my lady," he said as he wiped a particularly large clump of charred herbs and blood out of his eye. With a flick of his wrist, it flew off his fingers and hit the ground with a splat. "What's next?"

"Now, we only need wait until the dawn of Lughnasadh. In a few short hours, James, he will be mine again. He will be all mine!"

CHAPTER EIGHTEEN

After a stop for gas and a quick stretch before dawn, they climbed back in the van and continued on. Fortunately for Rowan's sanity, Trudy had picked up an inspirational romance novel in Red Bluff. It was not a bodice ripper with loose women and dangerous strangers. This one contained good Christian morals. Trudy tried to read about Mary Sue Helen explaining to Henry that she did love him but could never be with him since he was already married to his mad wife, but she had difficulty pretending she couldn't hear the sacrilegious conversations around her. Rowan had been telling stories from long ago to the three girls and gave them magical instruction to help them develop their individual "powers," whatever that meant. Trudy was worried and scared, trapped in a car full of weirdos who talked about magic and monsters as if they were everyday occurrences. All that talking she did to Rowan must've gone in one ear and out the other, for here he was talking nonsense again. She still didn't believe any of it. Vampires. What nonsense! They must be pulling her leg, trying to scare her, the spiteful little brats. She knew they didn't like her, and she certainly didn't like them. Best that this entire thing was over, so she could go back home.

Back to normal life.

Max had the wheel for the home stretch which would be three hours, if traffic cooperated and they didn't get lost. Rowan sat in the passenger seat to entertain the three girls; Ralph sat next to Trudy in the back.

That was fine with her.

Better than that red-haired, tattooed heathen. At least he wasn't wearing that dirty dress anymore, but then he could have found a shirt that fit him properly. The one they put him in looked as though it was painted on, like he was proud to show off his strong arms and all those evil tattoos. Disgusting.

She put her book down, unable to concentrate, and turned to Mr. Ferguson with a smile. He was busy scribbling notes in a journal. At least this Mr. Ferguson seemed halfway normal, if you could call a science nerd normal. So he was awkward and shy, at least he wasn't the witch she suspected Max to be.

They were all witches.

What had she gotten herself into?

Maybe this was all an elaborate ruse to kidnap her. After all, she only had their word that Rex had engaged in assault and theft. Maybe she should go to the police. But if Rex had done those things, however unlikely, then he would go to prison. She couldn't let that happen to her little boy. He was all she had left in the world.

She knew she needed these people to help her rescue her son, but they frightened her. She didn't want to understand them. They had no place in her world. They were dangerous, like terrorists or criminals. They didn't obey the rules.

They were, however, the only ones who could get her son back. She would just have to put up with them for the time being. When this was all over, she decided, she would take her son far away from the hippies and devil worshippers of California. Nothing was keeping her there anymore. They would move back to Texas, where people still feared God and didn't get mixed up with all this heathen magic. Yes. Texas. They would start a new life.

After that was all set, she tried to read again, but it was no use. She gave up with an involuntary snort of disgust and put the book in her bag, folded her arms across her chest, leaned her head back, and pretended to sleep. Maybe if she pretended long enough she really would fall asleep. She didn't get near enough last night, and this van was terribly uncomfortable.

But since her own thoughts had quieted down, Rowan's words snuck in.

"Gifts can be a blessing, but not always," he said. "What they always are is a responsibility. Gifts are provided by the earth, this living planet that we are all a part of. They are given to fulfill a need, and as such, they should be used to further the well-being of this world, which is a mother to us all."

Oh! Please! thought Trudy. *All gifts flowed from God!*

This world is a place of wickedness. It's a proving ground where people are tested. When the rapture happens, the righteous would be separated from the Evil. The faithful like her would be taken up into paradise. On Judgment Day, the evil followers of Satan and those seduced by his powers would be condemned to an eternity in the fires of hell. And it was no better than they deserved. Just listen to the garbage being spewed by this so called wizard.

"By using your gifts for the good of all, you become more connected to everything around you. And that connection is the conduit through which power is given to you. Therefore, the better the use of your gifts, the stronger those gifts and their wielders shall become."

Trudy scoffed. Is that supposed to be some sort of mamby-pamby-I'm-okay-you're-okay-zen-thing? It's just a bunch of nonsense dressed up to sound like wisdom. Why do they listen to him? That Maddy at least looks like she could put up an argument.

And Maddy did. "What about Fiana? She seems plenty powerful enough. And she isn't doing anything for anyone but herself."

Trudy noticed that just the mention of her name brought sadness into Rowan's eyes. His smile faded. She knew that look all too well. It was loss and grief and love. "When she first began," he explained, "and through all the years I knew her, she was a good person. She did much to the benefit of all around her. It was through these activities that she learned to harness and focus her powers. Later, after I became lost to her, her generous ways became twisted so that where once she nurtured a natural growth, she now feeds on the powers of others. She can wield great powers, but now she must steal it from others. The living power she takes is corrupted and consumed by her. It is a decidedly unhealthy way."

As if his magic was any cleaner, sniffed Trudy.

She decided that she must get some answers about what was going on from someone, so she turned to Ralph and asked quietly, "Who is this Fiana they keep speaking about?"

After all, he seemed to be the most logical among this freak show.

"She's Rowan's wife. Haven't we been through this?" His thoughts were obviously focused on something else, so his answer was absent minded at best.

Trudy tried to fit this into her understanding of how the world worked.

"Bad divorce then?"

"No, they're still married."

"Then, what's the problem?"

"She's a vampire steeped in evil who wants to do the same to him, but he's against it."

"Oh. The vampire nonsense again."

"It's not nonsense, Trudy. Why won't you believe it?"

"Because it's absurd! Honestly! You call yourselves educators. I'm writing a letter."

Ralph sighed and turned back to his notes.

She didn't want to know more anyway. In fact, she didn't want to know as much as she had just learned. Fortunately, she didn't have to believe it. She refused to believe it.

CHAPTER NINETEEN

Trudy waited outside the rented office of The Eternal Cleansing of the Desert Wind in the small town of Gerlach, Nevada. She figured having an office in BFE was a good way to keep distance between the outside world and the secrets this so-called organization wished to hide.

The sign on the glass office door said it opened at nine. Trudy looked at her watch. It read eight forty-five. Fifteen more minutes. She tapped her foot and looked around. Shifted her weight from foot to foot. Looked at her watch again. "Too early," she said to herself. "They dumped me off here too early." She had already been waiting for another fifteen, and she wasn't the only one.

A young man sat on a travel-worn backpack, reading *One Flew Over the Cuckoo's Nest*, and Trudy figured he must know about that first hand. She kept her distance from him because he needed a bath and a haircut. Standing well away from both he and Trudy, a worried looking middle-aged couple talked quietly to each other. Trudy guessed they were here for the same reason as she was: one of their children had been sucked into the lies. She wondered how long it would be before Cuckoo Boy's parents would be there.

She overheard a little of their conversation, despite their hushed tones. They had less of an idea about what they were walking into than she did and were even less prepared. Trudy looked at her watch. The minute hand hadn't budged since the last time she looked. She shook her arm and then put it up to her ear to hear if it ticked. It did.

"Watched pot and all that," she mumbled to herself and decided to join the middle-aged couple rather than Cuckoo Boy.

"Good morning." She smiled at them in an attempt to show companionship in adversity, as she moved closer to them, careful to make a wide circle around Cuckoo Boy.

"Good morning," the woman replied warily. They did not return her smile or feigned friendliness.

"I'm guessing you're not here to become a member." Trudy crossed her arms and cast a significant, judgmental look at the kid.

"No. That's not why we're here."

They didn't want to give any personal information, and Trudy could hardly blame them. This was all rather frightening and strange. Her stomach filled with butterflies at the thought of having to pretend to be a convert. She could never pull it off. She knew that now in this moment. The thought of it alone was way too stressful. If she couldn't even lie to these people, how was she supposed to make those in charge believe her? Perhaps she should be as honest as she could without jeopardizing herself or her son. It might make her task harder, but it would probably deflect suspicion if she seemed to be open about her reason for being here. But they had all decided together what to do. Would this mess up the plan? What was she worried about? She didn't owe those freaks anything. This was about her and her son. Period. The only thing on her mind was safety for herself and her son. The rest of them could go, well, you know where. Which is exactly where they would be going. No doubt about that!

Then there was this couple who were probably here for the same purpose as she: the retrieval of a child. Maybe they could bond over that. She wondered what Jesus would do in this situation, and she figured He'd tell the truth. So that's exactly what she did.

"I'm looking for my son. I'm Trudy." She held out her hand in a rather bold move to strangers in a dusty, foreign place.

The man shook it politely. "Hi. Bob Wilson; this is Judy."

"Hello," said Judy, shaking Trudy's hand as well.

"Yes, we want to see our daughter. See that she's okay," said the man. "She's been gone a month, and we've just discovered where she is. She's only eighteen, barely an adult. We just want to know she's okay. That's all."

"And bring her home if we can," added his wife. A silent tear rolled down her cheek, and Trudy turned away. Public was no place to display emotion. Any good southern woman knew that. But it was rather a traumatic situation, not knowing if your child was okay or not.

"Do you think there'll be any problem seeing our kids?"

They were beginning to relax towards her, sensing that she was a companion in adversity rather than an unknown threat.

"There's not supposed to be. We called ahead and made an appointment. The lady was very nice, polite and professional. She said that they encourage family members to visit and emphasized that this was in no way a cult. That it is a retreat center for those following their path, and followers are free to leave whenever they choose."

Trudy found this news encouraging but knew better than to trust it. If even half of what those freaks said was true about this Fiana character, there were lies aplenty to go around. The vampire stuff, of course, was nonsense. They were all quite obviously delusional.

These were the kind of friends she needed. Wholesome folk, not witches and wizards and pagan freaks. What was the world coming to? First, evolution in schools, denying her boy the truth of creationism. Then, guns and school shootings. Now, pagans and witchcraft? Yes. Back to Texas as soon as Rex was safe. She has now seen evil. Looked it in the eye, so she would be on her guard. She would make what friends she could, but trusting them? Never.

"That sounds a lot more hopeful than I was led to expect," she said.

Judy still looked uncertain despite her previous statement. "Why? What have you heard? Do you believe it?"

Trudy tried to sound casual in her reply, not only to soothe these nice people, but also to soothe her own nerves. With a dismissive wave of her hand, she said, "Oh, just a lot of nonsense really. Rumors and gossip. You know how it is."

"Have you talked to other parents then?"

"Actually, it was some kids. Their crazy uncle ran off to this cult or commune or whatever it is, or was maybe abducted by them, depending on which one you talk to."

"Oh. Well, they're just kids. They have a tendency towards hyperbole. You can't put too much stock in what they say."

"I guess not. But it's just not like my son to run off like that. He's a good boy. God-fearing boy."

"Well it's hard to tell what these young people are thinking these days. How old is he?"

"Fifteen. Just turned back in May."

"Oh. Well, that's different. He's underage. They have to send him home."

"Do they?"

"Of course. He's a minor. If they tried to keep him, it would be kidnapping."

"I suppose so, but what if he doesn't want to come home? And he's rather big for his age. No one really can make him do anything he doesn't want to."

"Why wouldn't he want to? Come home, I mean."

The butterflies returned. No. This time they were more like pelicans or frantic sparrows pecking at her insides. Images streamed back: she and Frank screaming at each other and Rex storming out of the house; her talking for hours on Skype with Andre in Paris; Cullen leaving and moving into a mansion. She realized that she had been so wrapped up in her own life that she had been neglecting Rex.

"I suppose there's not much of one to come home to," she said, tearing up. "I just divorced his father. The bastard had been cheating on me for years. He even had another son, the same age as mine. I just found out recently. Fifteen years, Judy! Fifteen years of lies. How do I rewrite my reality for over a decade?"

"Oh, my dear. I'm so sorry," Judy took a step back as if this was too much information to process on top of everything they were going through, especially from a stranger. It was a gesture of self-protection, not rudeness. She tried to be kind, so she spoke to just a little sliver of it. The part she could deal with at this moment. "Divorce can be hard on the kids. They don't know how they fit into the world all of a sudden. Some of them take it bad, but I'm sure he'll come around and understand that it's for the best. It sure sounds like it."

"Yes, I know. He's a good boy. I just worry about him."

"That's what parents do." Judy looked like she was getting ready to ask another question, but then they heard the door being unlocked and everyone turned to face the building.

A woman in a tailored business suit had just opened the door from the inside and smiled a welcome.

"Good morning, please come in."

They all filed in and stood expectantly, their eyes on the woman. She addressed the middle-aged couple first. "Mr. and Mrs. Wilson, I presume? I've been expecting you. Please go on into the office and have a seat. I'll be with you in a moment." She pointed them down the hall to a door open on the right before turning back to Trudy and the vagabond boy. "If you two would like to have a seat in the lobby here, I will be with you shortly. There are coffee and doughnuts on the sideboard. Please help yourself." She then busied herself pulling open the blinds to let in the bright morning sunlight. Trudy followed Cuckoo Boy into a waiting room with half a dozen plastic chairs, the promised coffee, and a low table displaying neatly arranged reading material all based around the cult in question.

With a snort toward the pamphlets, Trudy got herself some coffee, black, and added a healthy slug from the emergency flask of vodka she kept in her purse. She sat in the chair nearest the inner office, but she couldn't overhear any of their conversation.

The Cuckoo Boy had brought in his backpack and was once again sitting on it in the corner, despite the number of available chairs, still reading his Cuckoo book.

Trudy downed her first cup of coffee before standing to stretch, still stiff from sleeping in the van. Sure that the boy was nose-deep in his novel, she went for another cup of coffee and vodka, swigging directly from the bottle while she stirred the spike into the steamy blackness. Her mood steadily improved with each added nip. She stowed the half-empty bottle back into her purse, vowing to save some for later. Who knew what the rest of the day would hold?

After about thirty minutes and three more cups of spiked coffee, the office door down the hall opened and the Wilsons came out. Judy was drying her eyes with a white handkerchief, and Bob wore an expression of complete defeat. They passed through the waiting area without a word and went directly outside. The well-dressed woman then turned and asked Trudy back to the office. Cuckoo Boy hardly looked up from his novel when he saw the woman gesturing to Trudy.

"Good morning. Nancy Franklin. How may I help you?"

"Hi, Nancy. My name is Gertrude Samuels." Trudy extended her hand and Nancy shook it.

"Come in, Ms. Samuels, and let's chat." Holding her purse protectively against her body, Trudy followed Nancy into her office.

"Please, call me Trudy."

"Okay, Trudy, what can I do for you?"

Nancy's office was sterile. Bare walls. No personal effects whatsoever. One single poster advertising The Eternal Cleansing nonsense. Nothing more. Nancy sat down and folded her hands on her organized, sparse desk and looked at Trudy intently. After taking a seat across from her, Trudy continued, "I'm looking for my son Rex. I understand that he has joined your organization."

"Really? Are you sure?"

"Yes. Pretty sure. He went to some place called The Eternal Cleansing of the Desert Wind." Trudy pointed to the poster on the wall. "This is the office for that retreat, is it not?" Trudy said the word "retreat" with added emphasis, implying that it was anything but.

"This is, but everyone comes through this office first, Ms. Samuels, to be registered and accounted for, in the event of family coming to join them. Although hundreds have been through here, I certainly would've remembered a unique name like Rex. It means "king," right?"

"That's right. So you say Rex isn't here? Maybe he didn't come through the office. He's working with the organizer, Fiana. She's some kind of leader or something? He said she was an angel who appeared to him several times over the past few months. But, you know kids. They tend toward hyperbole." Trudy didn't know what that word meant, but since Judy said it and it sounded rather intelligent, she used it again.

Nancy blinked twice and then resumed—Trudy couldn't think of another word to describe it—her predatory stare. Trudy found it hard to tell what was really going on under her mask of pleasant professionalism, but she was quite sure this woman, and all of this, wasn't what it seemed. It was all too...perfect. Besides, these professional types always made her suspicious. They were too clever by half, able to twist your thoughts around with arguments that sounded reasonable while they robbed you blind. And *this organization* especially, hiding behind some spiritual cause or something. Sacrilege on top of a con.

"Well, I can check my database in case my memory fails me, Ms. Samuels. If he is with us,he will be listed there."

"Do that, please. And do call me Trudy."

"Of course, Trudy."

Nancy's long, perfectly painted, fingernails made tapping sounds as she typed on the keyboard. She sat perfectly erect. Her make-up was perfect. Her desk was perfect. Everything was perfect. It was all just too perfect. *She's probably just humoring me,* Trudy thought. *She thinks she's too smart for a country girl like me, but she will soon learn her mistake. She doesn't know what I'm capable of. After all, this country girl has been to Paris.*

Trudy took another sip from her coffee cup and gloated, starting to feel like she was above Nancy and all this nonsense. She'd collect Rex and they'd go back to Texas. That's right.

"I don't see the name listed. Could he have used a pseudonym?"

Blank stare.

"Another name? Could he have registered under another name?"

"I don't see why he would, but he is a minor who has disappeared and was last seen in the company of this Fiana. If you can't help me, then I'm sure the FBI can, or maybe the ATF. After all, this could be seen as kidnapping, Ms. Franklin."

Hard ball. That's what these professional types understood.

Nancy's cold smile never faltered, not even at the unveiled threat. Rather, she maintained a detached demeanor.

"Now, now, don't you worry, Trudy. I'm sure I can help you find your son. If you would like to visit out retreat center personally, I can arrange transportation for you. If he's with us and somehow evaded checking in here, he would be there. We don't keep any secrets. There is simply no need, so you will be free to walk around and inspect everything at your leisure. You will also be able to meet everyone who's there. So even if your son used a fake name you can recognize him and take him home with you if you both so choose. Will that be okay?"

Trudy nodded. "That sounds reasonable." She was getting what she wanted, and she hadn't needed to lie. A little righteousness went a long way. And maybe the freak squad had exaggerated the danger. Maybe, she could just find her son and take him home. Let them deal with their own mess. After all, it was obvious they lacked her righteous path and integrity. They wanted to lie and sneak around. They wanted to plot and get revenge. But the straight and narrow was her way, and she would follow The Lord down that path over a flame-haired wizard any day.

"We have a van heading out to the resort at ten. That's in about fifteen minutes. If you would like to wait in the back, I will make sure you get a seat. Just step this way." She led Trudy out a back door and into a parking lot. Empty, save a black van. The Wilsons were already seated on a bench underneath a cast concrete shade canopy. Bob held Judy's hand and patted it with tenderness. Her eyes were red-rimmed from crying, and Bob's expression still held that fear. Trudy wondered what Nancy had said as she joined them. They looked as though they didn't want to talk, and neither did Trudy. She figured there was no sense in cultivating a bond or friendship. This would all be over soon, and she'd never see them again. No need to waste the energy, so they all sat in silence until they boarded the van. Cuckoo Boy climbed aboard just in time and sat directly in front of Trudy. He really, really did need a bath. Trudy managed to sneak a text off to the freak squad before they left. Who knows if there would be cell service where they're going?

Max put the iPhone back in her pocket.

"Trudy said she's on the way to the compound. She's with another recruit and some parents looking for their kid. She doesn't think cell phones work out there, but if we get close enough we can use the radios."

"Should we try to follow the van out there?" Maddy asked.

"No, let's wait until late afternoon," said April. "I can keep track of her with my special sight, so we'll know where she is. But we should give her some time to find things out. We really don't know what we're going into. I'm sure that Fiana is expecting us. It could be a trap."

"That's a good idea," agreed Aidan. "It will give us some daylight, but will also let us wait until darkness if we need to do some snooping around."

"Since when can you do that with your visions?" Maddy poked April in the arm rather hard, as if she had purposely kept this secret from her, her best friend.

"Ow! Since I've been doing my homework and practicing. Unlike some of us." Maddy hadn't been keeping up with her exercises to strengthen her ability. It was harder for her, after all, taking on other's feelings. Well, she did practice some, like on her mom yesterday, but her efforts were sporadic at best. It was just a lot to deal with, and she didn't want to spiral down again. Best to keep control of these things.

"So what is the plan," asked Ralph who felt like he'd missed some key component. "We're just have to await developments and react to them. Wouldn't it be better to take the initiative here?"

"The plan is, we find out as much as we can from Trudy's reconnaissance. Then we go in and rescue everyone."

"Do you really think we can trust her. I mean, surely you all noticed her level of denial about all this. How many times have we told her about Fiana? And each time she acts like it's the first time she's heard the word vampire."

"Give the poor woman a break, honey," Max said. "Her son has gone missing and her husband left her and she's just been bombarded with the existence of supernatural creatures. She's likely in shock."

"My point exactly. And she's taking point? I'm just not so sure it's the best course of action."

"April's right," Rowan said. "Fiana probably expects us. I've felt a definite pull since last night. She's calling me, likely with spell work. And with it being Lughnasadh and a full moon, there is extra power behind it."

"Why didn't you say something?" Max asked.

"I did not wish to worry you. I don't know what it means yet, but she's up to something."

"Lughnasadh," Maddy said. "That's the beginning of the harvest. A time for trial marriages and the start of August, the month of truces. See. I do homework, too."

"Very good, Madeline," Rowan said. "That's right. We were first handfasted for a year and a day on Lughnasadh before we were permanently joined that Samhain night." Sadness and regret crossed Rowan's features, and he got very quiet.

"So there is something brewing," Aidan said. "Of course there is. It was foolish to think this would be easy. Not that I did, but I also didn't expect this. Are we prepared enough?"

"I guess we'll soon see," Maddy said. "Why are we trusting Trudy again?"

"We're not," Aidan explained. "But, there is possibility she will give us some useful info before she runs off or betrays us. Right now we are on the same side, but it's anyone's guess how long that will last."

CHAPTER TWENTY

Trudy stared around in amazement, awestruck at the sight of this desert paradise. Considerable effort over the years had been spent in creating a palace in the wilderness. As far as the eye could see, irrigated fields lay throughout the former desert to the east of the palace. The natural sandstone cliffs had been carved into rooms and terraces. An opulent balcony centered the stone façade, high above their heads. Gardens of myriad blooms and savory herbs surrounded the tourists as they made their way past an ornate fountain in the center of the court. Scores of people milled about, all of whom appeared to be mumbling to themselves.

The pale young driver with his face full of acne led them into the coolness of a vast interior hall. Darker than the bright desert sun, the interior was lit with what looked like flickering gaslights. An immense statue sat in the center of the three-story-high chamber. Surrounded by a large fountain, similar to the one outside, the beautiful stone woman dominated the hall. Twenty feet she rose, a stylized goddess of the wind. Clad in diaphanous robes of stone, she was a still life of gale forces. Her stone curls forever set in perfection. The scent of incense hung heavy in the air. Great stone braziers placed strategically around the room sent up an aromatic fog which encumbered Trudy's mind with a heavy weight.

And there she was.

From the freak squad's and Rex's descriptions, Trudy recognized the woman seated on the fountain's stone perimeter. With a dangling hand, Fiana played idly with the water in the pool. She didn't look as fearsome as she had been portrayed, but fear gripped Trudy anyway. Her hand went up to clutch the silver cross hanging around her neck, and she whispered prayers to her Lord. The others gathered near Trudy, and Fiana stood up before them and spoke in a language that wasn't English. It wasn't French, either. It was the most bizarre combination of sounds Trudy had ever heard. The cross warmed in her hand, causing her to drop it, but then she felt naked without it. She gathered it between her fingers again, explaining away the warmth on the desert air. That's all it was, right?

What was going on?

A dizziness overtook Trudy, and she had to focus on a crack in the sandstone to regain her balance. Somehow disconnected from their surroundings, her fellow passengers listened to Fiana speak with rapt attention, but Trudy still couldn't understand a word she said. It sounded like nonsense or some ancient foreign language. Maybe it was that language the terrorists used. Somehow she was out of the loop, because she found nothing interesting about the unintelligible words. Rather, she felt quite bored. She looked at her surroundings with disinterest.

More classically styled statues lined the walls of the chamber. Trudy leaned forward, as if it could help her make out the details, but her eyes were drawn back to the main fountain statue rising above her. Its eyes began to glow, like tiny blue light bulbs were in the statue's eye sockets. Then the eyes of all the statues glowed blue, answering their stone mother in the middle.

Time seemed irrelevant.

Nothing seemed real, nothing except the warm silver of the cross she held in her fingers. She stopped looking at the blue statues' eyes. They tried to charm her. She could feel those blue eyes penetrating into her very soul.

Dizzy again.

She focused all her attention on her cross, clinging to it as if it were a life buoy.

Fiana's words turned more passionate, determined, louder.

Trudy clamped her eyes shut and squeezed the cross as the rest of the universe slipped past her.

Awash in confusion.

Any understanding dissolved into incomprehension.

Reality lacked substance.

Only the cross clutched tightly in her hand anchored her to herself.

And then the words stopped.

The world came back into alignment.

She looked around, and everything seemed as it was when they had entered.

Except her companions.

Their eyes loosely focused on nothing, empty of any independent consciousness. Other than that vacant look, Trudy couldn't have articulated how else they had changed. But they had indeed changed. A wave of pure terror shot through her soul, and then she understood. As if someone had placed the clarity of thought into her mind, recognition blossomed. They had become soulless, devoid of the critical element that made them individuals. The very thing that made them human.

And she had been spared. Her Lord and Savior had saved her from this demon disguised as a beautiful woman. She wanted to run and hide, but what would this bride of Satan do to her if she realized she had been unaffected? She had to try to act like everybody else.

Fiana stood before them, pleased. Thankfully she had turned away after her incantation to talk with a handsome dark-haired man. His hair was tied back with a single black ribbon. Trudy hadn't seen him approach. He must've come in when her eyes were shut. She suppressed a gasp when he turned around. A knife stuck straight out of his chest, but he still walked around. Quickly lowering her gaze to match the others, she followed when Fiana beckoned them. Leading them towards the rear of the chamber, Fiana took them through a set of large double doors, solid slabs of dark wooden planks jointed closely and carved with braids and knots, which swung open on their own when she approached.

Trudy stopped breathing as she realized that she had fallen completely out of her depth. Realizing she would be discovered, she gasped and began to hyperventilate. Her breath came faster in the fear that bubbled up from her stomach. Sour vodka and black coffee gurgled up into her throat.

What had happened? How had she gotten here? The rules she had lived by her entire life no longer applied.

Only one remained.

She had been saved from whatever had affected the others. Her faith had saved her. Regaining control of her breath, she kissed the cross. She would cling to it as a protection in this valley of evil. With its strength she would persevere. Following God's path, she would find her son. Had he kept his faith? Or fallen under the witch's spell?

She feared the worst.

Unknown to her, while she had slept the night before, Rowan had cast charms of protection upon it. They would have been much more efficacious if he'd had his wand, but they were strong enough for the immediate need.

The interior doors led to a winding staircase which they all ascended and emerged into another immense audience hall. This was the room with the balcony Trudy had noticed before. It looked like the throne room for royalty she had seen on TV.

Fiana ascended the three steps leading up to her throne, turned with an air of importance, and sat down. The man with the hilt of a dagger protruding from his chest stopped at her right hand. From this high seat Fiana gazed down upon her new converts, three standing in adoration, and Trudy, trying to contain her terror and mimic the expressions of the others, from what she could see in her peripheral vision. Sweat streamed down the sides of her face and into her eyes, stinging them.

Fiana pointed to her.

"That one. Bring her here."

Trudy's heart plummeted. She clutched her cross and prayed silently, reciting *Oh my God! Oh my God!* over and over inside her head. Willing her feet to work, she thought she'd make a run for it, but her legs wouldn't move. A piteous whimper escaped her lips as two burly men, who Trudy hadn't noticed when she had entered because they had flanked the doors, stepped forward and grasped her by her upper arms, lifting her off the ground. Her legs, now working, flailed in the air trying to get away, but they carried her with little effort closer to Fiana, who gazed at her with curiosity.

"You intrigue me, simple woman. How is it that you are immune to my spell? There is nothing fey about you. Yet you resist me completely. How is this?"

Now Trudy's lips didn't work. She wanted to chide this pretentious woman for calling her simple. Who did she think she was? But she could produce no sound other than another whimper, a manifestation of the utter terror bubbling up from her gut.

I asked you a question! Be so good as to respond! I do not tolerate insolence." Menace and consequences lurked within the soft tones.

The answers made it past Trudy's fear, bursting like a pierced boil from her trembling lips, "Jesus protects me."

Fiana smiled. "Is that so?"

"That's right. Through his grace I am saved."

Delight dominated Fiana's ire for the time being. "That I highly doubt. I suppose he helps you as well with other aspects of your life? Motherhood. Success. Maintaining domestic bliss and all that? How's that working out for you?"

Trudy winced. To mock The Lord in this way took a truly evil person—or demon. She had seen for herself now that this Fiana really did practice black magic, and possessed a cruel personality, unlike any she'd ever seen in person. This couldn't be happening. It was straight out of a movie, or straight out of the Old Testament.

As much as she disliked Cullen's friends, she admitted that they were correct on their assessment of this woman. Trudy had made the grave mistake of underestimating her, and it didn't look like she'd have the chance to make the same mistake twice. She was in danger, and so was her son.

Fiana motioned for the men to set Trudy down, and as soon as she was free, Trudy's hand went once again to the cross around her neck. "Though I walk through the valley of the shadow of death, I shall fear no evil," she recited aloud.

"Yes, yes, very amusing, but tell me, if you did not come to join me then why have you come into my domain? What is it you seek here?"

The eyes Fiana bent upon her pulled the truth from her. Again, Trudy felt compelled to answer. "I'm looking for my son, Rex."

Fiana laughed in delight. "How delicious. Are you his precious mother? How absolutely wonderful. Oh, but I must think upon this. Did you know that he is a most loyal servant? Unlike these mesmerized minions you see here, he follows me willingly, dedicated to me heart and soul." She put such emphasis and intonation on that last word that it made Trudy's skin crawl. "But you fail to follow me either way. A mystery I don't have time to untangle at the moment, but my curiosity is trumping my inconvenience, so I'll just put you in storage for now. Kill you later. I believe the room next to my former servant is free. Why don't you stay there while I attend to more immediate concerns. We will speak again soon. After I've had a little chat with your son."

The men once again grabbed Trudy, lifting her.

"Wait," Fiana said. "I sense something." Rising from her throne, she came before Trudy and touched her cheek with icy fingers, trailing down her cheek to her throat. As her manicured nails grazed Trudy's jugular, she licked her red lips. Then, with a quick jerk, tore the cross from her neck.

"No!" Trudy screamed.

"Yes. I taste my husband on this. He protected you, not your precious *lord*. As if. Take her."

It was not a suggestion. The two men holding Trudy man-handled her away.

Down.

Down.

Down.

The men carried her, kicking and pleading, through far-from-elegant passages and hallways. Through dark ways leading ever downward into darker places, they took her into what could only be recognized as a dungeon. A large, shirtless man in dirty cargo shorts, who wore the same blank gaze as the guards, unlocked one of the iron doors cut into the rock wall, and Trudy's guards thrust her into a bare cell, twelve foot square. They slammed the door behind her and slid the bolt into place.

She looked around in the semi-darkness at her new accommodations. No bed. No chair. Not even a cot or a pile of straw. The sole furnishing was a plastic five gallon bucket, empty. Surely it wasn't meant to be a commode? Trudy pushed herself into the far corner and sank to her knees, sobbing. The panic returned, and this time she let it come. Gasping for air, she collapsed onto all fours and tried to breathe and wished to die in all the same moment. Her purse slipped off her arm and fell on the ground, spilling its contents. As the anxiety subsided, for it would do her no good, she sat up on her knees and prayed, projecting her voice out toward the solitary window way out of her reach. Then a thought came to her. She looked down at the mess her purse had purged, finding the answer to her prayers.

"Thank you, Jesus."

She picked up the cell phone thingy Ralph had given her. Certainly there was no signal here, not this deep underground. But he had said it also had a two-way radio function that might work. Let the geek come through for her now. Please.

She tried Channel 3 first, just as Ralph had instructed. Nothing. Must be too far underground. Just to be sure, she tried the other channels, and, to her great surprise, Channel 1 answered. "Praise the Lord," she said.

"Well. I'm no lord, but I'm happy to hear from you anyway!" said a jolly voice, almost in stereo. "To whom do I have the pleasure of talking?"

She could hear the voice clearly through the phone, but she could hear it through the air as well, only fainter.

"This is Trudy Samuels. Who is this?"

"Fa-bu-lous! Trudy! My dear!" boomed the voice, inside and out. "What a pleasant surprise. This is Moody. How are you?"

Rage flared within her, and all her pious presence left her. "How am I? How do you think I am? I'm locked in a hole underground! And this is all your fault. Somehow, this is all your fault; I just know it. You and the rest of your freak squad."

"Ah, that would be why I can hear you so clearly. You must be in the adjoining cell," he said, ignoring the rest.

"Adjoining cell? Oh, great. A lot of help you'll be then."

"Don't despair my dear. I'm just biding my time until the time is ripe. The worlds are not quite aligned. But they soon will be. Oh yes, my dear, they soon will be. But tell me, how is it that you are here? Yes! How are you down here, my dear?"

"Never mind that. It's irrelevant. How are we going to get out of here?"

"Patience! Patience, my dear, all in good time. And it is quite relevant, I dare say! Any information you have may assist me completing that very task. Yes, indeed. So, if you will be so good as to tell me your story, I will listen patiently."

"Well," she said, calming down. "I guess I have nothing better to do in here."

"Quite right! Quite right, my dear!"

She decided that talking to someone, even the lunatic freak Moody, calmed her. Even made her smile a little. So absurd and chipper. Here they both were, locked up in a dungeon, and he even made her smile with his infectious optimism. Was this another spell?

"Oh, all right." She turned the bucket over for a very uncomfortable seat and told him the whole story in detail. He asked few questions, only about the rest of his family and friends, but he did seem particularly interested in the spell Fiana had cast and the statues with the glowing eyes. He had her describe it again in detail. And then again.

"Don't worry, my dear. You have been most helpful. I now have a better understanding of the situation. When the time comes all will be set aright."

His words of comfort helped some, even if she took them with more than a few grains of salt. No, actually, they didn't help nearly enough. Her irritation returned. "What can you do? You're locked up just like me."

"Patience, my dear! Patience! That is the watch word, my dear Trudy. Study calm. Find peace. All will come right in the end. I've been around a bit longer than you. Yes! Just a bit longer, and I have seen how these things go. Trust me."

Being talked down to like a child angered her further. "Trust you? You're insane! And not that much older than me. How dare you condescend!"

Moody chuckled. "Appearances can be very deceiving my dear. When I was young, Yeshua bin Josef had yet to be born. I had been around for many centuries before I met Fiana over one thousand years ago. I am one of the old ones, a relative of the Danann, and understand the old laws better than Fiana can hope to. The time of truce is nigh. When that time comes, all will change. Be patient."

Trudy put the phone away, irritated at how she had become surrounded by lunatics and captured by some kind of demon woman. This just would not do. Moody actually sounded as if he believed himself, which just proved how loopy he really was. They all were insane. The entire freak squad.

She scoffed at the idea that he could be so ancient.

Although, said a small nagging doubt, Fiana did turn out to be an evil witch just like they had said.

She did her best to banish this voice.

Who was this Yeshua Bin Joseph anyway? He sounded like a terrorist.

CHAPTER TWENTY-ONE

"Let's just go! All this waiting around is driving me insane. Further insane," Maddy clarified.

"We haven't heard from Trudy yet," Ms. MacFey said, looking up from her Kindle. "If we go in before she's ready, we could put her life in danger. Ours, too."

"But it's after three already! How much longer do we have to wait? What if she's already dead? What if she's trapped and needs rescuing? It's crazy just to wait here. Can't Rowan feel something? I'm too far away to feel, but maybe if we at least got closer I could."

"Fiana must have blocked herself from me. I have not felt her since Rex hit me on the head. I wish I could be of more help. I've brought this down on all of you."

"Not now, Rowan," Maddy said.

"Maddy!" Ms. MacFey scolded.

"Well! He's always about so sorry this and woe is me that, and I'm sick of it."

"Stop being so mean!" April said. "For someone with so much capacity for empathy, you're not being very compassionate. Show some respect."

"Look. We're all agitated from the heat. We should've brought more food, too," Ralph said.

"Yeah. And better food," Maddy said.

"Hey! At least I thought to bring something!" Aidan defended herself.

"Chips and crackers and cookies? Really?"

"Maddy. Stop it this instant," Ms. MacFey said.

Maddy crossed her arms and moved to a large orangish boulder away from the others. She plopped down and pouted.

"What's up with her?" Aidan asked.

"She's getting overwhelmed with all the high emotions and stress. Not an excuse for her behavior, just an explanation. This is hard for someone who feels as deeply as she does, and sometimes she just can't handle it," April explained. She spent more time with Maddy than anyone else did. "She doesn't mean to be mean or say those things. I'm so sorry, Rowan."

"It's all right. I guess I do have a tendency to repeat myself, but I feel responsible."

"Understandable," Ms. MacFey said, placing a hand on his shoulder.

Ralph stood up and turned away. "I'm going to go check on Maddy."

Max just sighed and shook her head.

"So where does that leave us in the plan?" Aidan asked. "Wait or go?"

"Wait. At least until sunset."

"Is that wise? I mean, Fiana is stronger at night, right? We're losing the element of surprise along with the power that Lughnasadh will bring."

"Do not concern yourself about that," Rowan said. The power of Lughnasadh will bring her more power, but it will also bring me and Marlin more power as well, especially with the full moon. We're lucky the full moon fell on Lammas."

"You don't sound too sure," Aidan said.

"What other choice do we have?"

"We'll give Trudy until sundown, then we'll make our move whether we hear from her or not.

"I shall not be able to resist the pull of Fiana's call after sunset, so at least I will have to go. Perhaps it is best that I go alone."

"Absolutely not," Max said. "You are never alone, Rowan, and I won't abandon Cullen. We'll go with you. It will take all of us to pull this off."

All in all prison is just plain boring, thought Trudy. She had finished her book by the light of the tiny window just in time, for the light faded fast. The novel had turned out to be less inspiring than she had hoped. Or maybe, it was because her situation lay far beyond the scope of its mundane audience. She considered trying to sleep, but didn't feel tired enough to manage it, especially on such a hard floor. The bucket had cut curves into her backside, and she had waited just about as long as she could. Grimacing, she realized that she might have to turn it over and make use of its other purpose. She cursed herself for having so much coffee, but after who knows how many hours, she just couldn't hold it anymore.

After humiliating herself, she tried pacing. It helped with her sore muscles, but not the boredom. The sun set, so the only thing still lighting her room was a small light bulb. Electric, not like those gaslights in the upper realms of the place. There seemed no way to shut it off, which would make sleeping even more difficult. She required total darkness to sleep, and she forgot to bring her eye shades. Another long night lay ahead.

She had failed.

She failed Rex.

She failed the freak squad.

She was useless in this dark cell all alone. If this self-proclaimed ancient wizard next door couldn't do anything, what could she possibly do?

She stared out of the small grill in the door and saw small, crisscrossed squares of light on the opposite stone wall, each represented an adjoining cell. The patch of light next to her own disappeared. Moody had turned his light off.

"Hey, how did you do that?" she called through the door.

"Why, my dear, I simply turned my bucket upside down and unscrewed the bulb. Careful though. It's rather hot. Nine parts heat to one light. Inefficient, I say! It's a wonder anyone still uses them. Still, better than the gaslights above. How strange to have part gas, part electric here. Knowing my lady, she likes the ambiance of the gaslights, but she, too, prefers comforts. And with electricity come comforts!"

"Are you going to sleep?"

"Oh no, my dear. I am in fact unscrewing the receptacle with a dime I happened to have in my pocket. You see, I kept my oath, so she could not despoil me of my possessions, as well as for my honor. It demands it, after all. Holy Mackrel-andy! It sure does! Still, she could not even take my wand, as that would negate the bond with which she binds me. So instead, she housed me in a chamber that renders all my magics ineffectual."

Trudy rolled her eyes in disbelief.

"You people really believe this nonsense. Don't you? How did I get in this predicament? Of all the foster kids I had to get that one. Okay. Fine. I'll play along with your little game. So, with all your "magical ability," you just sit there, doing what she wants?"

"My oath compels me. But she failed to prohibit mundane ingenuity. Ha! That's right! Ingenuity, my dear. So, I am attempting to make contact with our compatriots. They must know what we know, so they will be ready to foil her evil plans when our doors spring open. Ha ha! And spring open they will, my dear! Spring open they will!"

"By taking apart a light?"

"Indeed, the very thing. For inside this light fixture is a grounding wire that is linked to all the grounding wires in this complex, including the ones above ground. Even as we speak I am connecting it to the antenna adapter provided by our inestimable science teacher. With a bit of luck it will be sufficient."

A spark of hope flared within her breast. Maybe she would get out of this mess after all. She couldn't stand the man, nor the rest of them, but he did have a way of coming out on top. Just look at his house!

As they watched the sun set, they knew they had to act. Sweat dripped off Rowan's brow, his face and neck muscles tense from trying to keep from moving, from answering the call.

"It looks like his veins are going to burst," Maddy whispered to Aidan. Ralph had calmed her down earlier by offering a sympathetic ear and reassurances.

"I know. This must be torture for him. I think he is stronger than any of us know, except for poor Cullen."

"Maybe we should just wait until morning. I mean, she's more powerful at night, and all." This time Maddy had the voice of reason.

"You could be right," Max said, helping Ralph stow the last of their gear back in the van. "But we can't let Rowan and Cullen go in alone. We just can't. I really don't know what else to do. I suppose, the best we can. Everyone, climb in. Ready or not, here we go."

Ralph jumped as he felt his phone vibrate. "Wait, everyone. Someone's calling. Maybe it's Trudy. Shhhhh." But it wasn't a call. It was a text, and it said this:

Moody here. Do you read me?

"Hey, I just got a text from Moody."

Everyone crowded around him at the back of the van and looked over his shoulders as he typed back:

Yes, where are you?

The answer came quickly.

In her dungeon. The statue must be destroyed.

Remember the truce.

Come when it is time.

"How will we know when it's time?" Maddy threw her hands up in the air and stomped away from the others, breathing deep and trying to control her anger.

"Remember the truce?" asked Aidan. "What does that mean?"

Blank faces stared back at her.

"Lughnasadh." Rowan wiped the sweat from his face with the tail of his soaked t-shirt. "The truce. Fiana may actually honor it. But then, she may not. It is difficult to determine."

"Sounds like a trap." Maddy squatted low to the ground, hands flat against the dusty earth as if for balance. "Ask him why he went to her in the first place."

Ralph punched in the question.

I was compelled by an old oath. But that will soon end.

"And until then?" Maddy was getting worked up again.

Have you seen Trudy? Ralph's fingers darted over the virtual keyboard. Everyone held their breath for the response.

Cell next door.

"Well, a lot of good she turned out to be," Maddy said, crossing her arms again and giving up on her grounding exercise when she heard Aidan repeat the last text out loud.

"Never mind that. No time for judgments or squabbles." Aidan stomped her foot and glared at Maddy. "How does this truce thing work?"

Maddy rolled her eyes and pressed her hands flat against the ground again, breathing.

"Since time immemorial a sacred truce existed during the time of Lughnasadh. Friends and enemies alike would gather.

Disputes could be settled without recourse to violence. Many old feuds were ended in this way." Rowan's breath came in short bursts, and he squinted his eyes tight against the pain."

"Yeah, but the way things used to be isn't always how they are now."

"Times change, but people's natures change very little. Even in the days when Lughnasadh was first celebrated, there were those who broke the truce. Always to their own peril."

"If others have done it, then Fiana certainly will."

"I fear you are correct. But she takes great risk in doing so."

"How is this going to help us, then?"

"Moody suggests we take advantage of this time to approach Fiana openly and demand justice. For it is during this time of truce that leaders hold a feast and dispense justice to those who seek it. It is an approach with some merit. But there is more we need to know and much to consider."

"Wait just a minute. Are you suggesting we invite ourselves to dinner so she can poison our food or something? That hardly seems like a reasonable plan to me," Maddy said.

"I have to agree with her this time," April added.

"In traditional lore, those who break the truce are the ones to suffer. Take the example of Cian Druole."

"I might if I knew who he was."

"Enough!" Max said. "In the van! Everyone! Can't you see the man is in pain? Rowan, if we're at least moving toward the compound, will it help ease the suffering some?"

"It might. Thank you for your kindness. The physical pull is painful enough, and Cullen feels it as well. He hasn't stopped screaming inside my head since we stopped the van. Let us move and talk on the way. I shall tell you the story about Cian Druole."

Once they were on their way, Rowan's muscles relaxed and he stopped sweating. Max stroked his temples and soothed him until he assured her Cullen had stopped screaming.

Aidan sat in the front seat next to Ralph whose jaw was as tense as all of Rowan's muscles had so recently been.

"Better?" asked Maxine.

"Much better, thank you." Rowan sat up from Max's embrace and moved away from her. After a glance in the rear view mirror, Ralph relaxed as well. Maddy and April sat in the far back seat.

"Please tell us the story, Rowan. Anything to keep my mind off what we're going to face. I can't bear the nausea, and my heart is starting to race," Maddy said.

"Of course. Cian Druole. In a time long before my own he ruled over a holding in the Highlands, although not a very significant one. However, Cian's nature was of the kind that deluded himself into thinking his power and importance exceeded the reality of his reach. He possessed above-average intelligence, so he thought himself better than everyone else. Smarter. More handsome. More powerful. More true and more everything. And because he had so much skill in eluding responsibility for his actions through his skills at debating and taking the easy way, blaming others along the way, he could confuse his listeners with his rhetoric. He believed that rules did not apply to him. But like so many who break the rules, he made very sure that others followed them. Through masterful manipulation, they all believed in him and would do whatever he asked. They were under a spell of sorts. His charm, for why do you think they call it charming? Yes. Always be wary of those who are charming. It is dark magic, that. So Cian would demand powerful oaths from his followers, and they would take these oaths despite the potential damage to their families and themselves. Of some he even demanded the oath of Oberon."

"What's that?" April knew it was impolite to interrupt stories, but she was too curious to stay quiet.

"A powerful oath that lays a geas upon the giver to attend his liege at his castle whether he wishes to or no. One who had sworn such an oath, MaCuel by name, had been greatly wronged by Cian. Yet his oath compelled him to attend the Lughnasdha feast. There Cian taunted him. Teased him. Humiliated and dehumanized him in front of all the others. MaCuel, being bound by the truce, although he had seen through Cian's treachery, passed it off. Though inside he seethed with rage, he maintained a placid exterior, for the truce was in effect. Cian tried over and over, displaying his cruelty in ever increasing taunts. Yet nothing broke MaCuel's placid acceptance. Finally, driven to a rage beyond endurance by his failure, he seized up a knife from the table and hurled it at MaCuel, piercing his shoulder. At that instant, all oaths sworn to him and the entire fealty owed to him were no more, for he had broken the sacred truce and placed himself beyond all laws. Then everyone in the hall rose up laid their hands upon him and carried him out to a loch wherein dwelt a Fuath. There they did cast him. But yet they showed him mercy. So he would have some manner to defend himself, they left his weapons and armor upon him."

"Wouldn't that just cause him to sink faster?"

"Indeed, it did."

"Ah! I get Moody's intention! Tell me what to ask and I'll pass it along," offered Ralph.

"We need to make some clearer plans! I'm lost!" Aidan, very anxious about Moody, asked for further clarification. "What's he got planned? If you get something, please explain it to the rest of us."

"Max, take the wheel."

Ms. MacFey squeezed between the steering wheel and Ralph's lap.

"Keep your foot on the gas. We've already wasted enough time." Ralph moved to her former place next to Rowan, bent over his phone, and with thumbs moving in quick staccato over the virtual keyboard, continued to exchange information with Moody. He shook his head without taking his eyes from the small screen. "He doesn't say what's planned."

Maddy initiated her signature eye roll. "Great, so we're just supposed to trust him?"

Max sighed. "I don't see that we have much of a choice."

Ralph's phone buzzed again and again in the palm of his hand. "He's sending a constant stream of instructions."

"And if he's switched sides again?"

Rowan looked grave. "I don't think he has. Fiana has found some way to trap him, but I doubt she can regain his loyalty. Not after what he's seen. He has told me many stories. Stories I am loathe to believe about my beloved. He may seem like a silly, eccentric man, but you must remember he is one of the fey. He is far older than any of us and can be quite subtle if the fancy takes him."

"All right," interrupted Aidan, "we just don't have the time to doubt our friends at the moment. We're almost there, so let's assume he's on our side and see what he has to say."

CHAPTER TWENTY-TWO

Fiana sat upon her throne once more and watched the last traces of sunlight disappear behind the distant mountains. "How appropriate," she mused, "The new day begins with the fall of darkness outside and the rise of darkness in here. Lughnasadh comes. The time of the first harvest. And I have only begun. The greater harvest comes with Rowan. I can feel him growing ever closer. Lammas reaches its full strength with the descent into darkness and the rising of the full moon for a second night."

One of her more comely minions led her newest servant into the room. He did amuse her. How wonderful such ignorance had not been bred out of the human race in all this time. If anything, there were more and more idiots born every day. Because who else but the ignorant and blind would continue to bring life into this cycle of pain? Fine with her. More food.

She could not resist playing with a mind as malleable as Rex's. Since he believed so fiercely, he was immune to logical arguments and too dense anyway. The simplest emotional manipulation could divert his attention and fervor onto a new path. He could be led anywhere with the right technique. As a result, her game with him precluded any use of magic directly upon him. She manipulated him and bound him to her by force of her personality.

Words alone seduced him.

"Good evening, my sweet boy. Come, sit beside me. At my right hand where you belong. Oh! Don't you look handsome this evening?" She emphasized the word 'handsome' with an intonation that signified she meant anything but handsome, but Rex didn't catch it.

"Thank you, my angel!"

She had ordered him arrayed in the finest clothes. Not as a prince of old, nor even in a tailored suit. Neither would suit him. Nor would he understand or be comfortable in them. She had had him dressed in the latest fashion for young adults by the loudest names in the industry, all the way down to his Tony Hawk skate shoes. The figure he cut in his new finery could only be described as rotund. He shuffled forward, still awed by her magnificence. His natural demeanor portrayed this as surliness, but she could see beneath the arrogance to the truth within: emptiness and constant fear. Good.

"We have much to discuss, you and I," she continued. "You look simply delicious today, sweetheart. Do you know you are my favorite of all my followers? You, who brought me the wand. Only someone with such cunning and skill as you clearly have would have been able to complete such a task."

"Yes, my lady." He beamed.

"Sit! Sit! We shall rule this kingdom together. Just you and I." She smiled at him. Such a sweet morsel. She would have such fun with this one.

He sat on the low ottoman beside her throne and looked up at her with awe, as if the sun itself shone on his face when she gazed upon him.

"Tell me, my paladin, how do you find your new quarters?"

"Quarters? What do I need quarters for? Is there an arcade?"

"No. Your accommodations."

Nothing.

"Your rooms?"

"Oh! They're great. The servants are a bit stupid, but I guess that's why they're servants."

Fiana could not help but laugh out loud at this, but he would not know the intention behind such a laugh. He was far more simple than any servant, of course, which is why she didn't need to mesmerize him. "That's very perceptive of you, sweetheart. I can see you are a very clever young man."

Rex glowed in her praise.

"That is, of course, the reason I chose you." *Not so much.* "As we both know, the world is filled with evildoers." *Like me.* "They violate the morality common to all people for their own sinister ends." *Ditto.* "I am very concerned with the amount of wickedness in the world. It is my sacred purpose to destroy and punish this wickedness." *Well, to destroy and punish, anyway.* "And you are the one I have found worthy to assist me. Together we will work to make this a better world for all who deserve one." *And so few do.*

Rex nodded. Though a vociferous braggart by habit, Fiana's presence silenced Rex. He recognized her superiority and paid it homage. His soul fed upon every word she uttered. Her words and her love for him filled the emptiness inside him, for she spoke a truth that made sense out of a crazy world. He recognized, too, that only one as special as he was worthy to sit at her right hand. Only one as great as she understood him.

"In order to do that, we need to get rid of the evildoers and punish the wicked. We will cleanse the world of the unrighteous."

"My lady," James said rushing in to her throne room. "Your presence is needed down below."

"What?"

"Please, my lady. It's Moody. He's escaped."

Fiana charged past James in a flash of color and emerged in the chamber of the statue below just as the massive doors leading into it swung open of their own accord. Simultaneously, all the other doors leading to various other hallways and chambers swung open as well.

"What is the meaning of this?" she demanded, too shocked to act.

"Lughnasdh has come," declared Moody, striding into the chamber from the rear door. Trudy followed several hesitant steps behind him. James hissed and moved to intercept him, but Moody forestalled him with a raised hand.

"Peace. It is the time of truce. Lughnasadh has arrived. My lady, you summoned me here by invoking the Lughnasadh law. Therefore, you have bound yourself to these same laws. During the time of the feast, your doors shall be open to all. And all who crave justice can petition you for it."

Moody stood before her unafraid, and although her green eyes bore down on him, emanating the rage boiling within, he did not flinch. Trudy hid behind his girth and peeked out at the red-haired beauty.

Fiana's grimace of anger turned into a smile with a wink of her eye. "Indeed! You are correct!" She turned to her stunned followers around her, and with her eyes spread out wide, she exclaimed at the top of her lungs, "Moody Moody Marlin is correct! Bring on the feast!"

"Tell me again. How we're going to survive our childhood?" Maddy looked at the outer gates to Fiana's compound. A twelve foot high chain-link fence disappeared into the growing darkness in either direction. The road itself was flanked by pillars of cut stone, and the space between those was filled with a ten foot iron gate. Whoever had erected this fortress failed to provide a gap that even a small child could squeeze through.

Maddy's question went unanswered.

Ralph pulled an unassuming meter gadget out of his backpack, too ordinary for one of his own inventions, and held it close to the gate and then the fence. He frowned at the reading. "Both are electrified enough to kill."

Aidan sighed. "Hardly surprising, I suppose. Suggestions anyone?"

April put her sight-enhancing headgear on and began fumbling with the dials to adjust it. "Is there some way to short it out? Maybe with magic? Rowan?"

"I'm afraid not. Fiana's signature is all over it. This is not only protected with electricity, but the electricity is protected with its own magic."

"Well, if she wants you so badly, why is she making it so hard for you to get in?" Maddy asked.

"She wants to ensure she is in control to the last. She knows I can't resist the pull, so I must come. The pain, it's coming again. Cullen, it's all right. I know it hurts, but please don't scream." Rowan clenched his eyes tight as all his muscles tensed again.

"He has to keep moving forward," Ms. MacFey shouted. "Can't you see he's in pain? And Cullen, too! Do something. We have to do something fast, or she'll know we're all here!"

"How about digging under?" Aidan offered.

"Too dangerous, and without tools it would take all night." Ralph put his arm around Max to comfort her.

"That just leaves the pillars." With her special goggles, she could actually see better than the others in the fast fading light. "Really? Can we catch a break here?" April felt the pressure and reacted to Rowan's quickening breath.

"What?"

"There's all this broken glass embedded in the mortar. It's no use. He's going to have to go in on his own or explode, by the looks of it."

Rowan's veins bulged even more than they did before. Every muscle in his body tensed and his jaw was clenched in agony. Tears fell down both Max's and Maddy's faces as they felt his pain. Maddy, especially, controlled each breath and focused on the ground before her while she inched away from him, hoping that distance would ease the pain emanating from him into her very soul.

"I've got an idea," Aidan said. "Everyone stand back." She took off her boots and socks and threw them over the fence as far as she could then inched up to a pillar. As she approached, it began to glow, and so did she. By the time she reached it, she had burst into flame, causing the others to gasp in unison. White hot heat radiated from the girl, so the others hastily retreated and shielded their eyes against the glow. Aidan hugged the pillar for a moment, stretching her arms as far as they would go in both directions, then slowly, she began to climb, kicking her foot and pushing her hand into the stone as she did. After she reached the top, she turned around and descended down the other side, feet first.

Once on the ground her flame went out and she backed away.

"Come on!," she said while putting her socks and boots back on. "Let's move before Rowan explodes."

"You first, Rowan," Max said. "Movement helps."

As soon as Rowan took a step toward the compound, his pain subsided. Heat radiated from the stones though they cooled rapidly with the help of the evening breeze to the occasional snapping sound as the soft stone cracked from its ordeal.

"It's still too hot," he said. "It will burn us all."

"Hold on," Maddy said, digging through her backpack and coming up behind Rowan. Now that he had stopped hurting, so had she. Dropping her backpack on the ground, Maddy shot the hot stone with a stream from her super soaker. A loud hissing noise filled the air. Steam billowed. As it cooled, they saw that all the glass had been melted smooth. Aidan had even created hand and toe holds into the stone. "That should do it. Get going, Rowan. The pain is returning. I can feel it, too, remember."

For the first time in as long as he could remember, Jimmy felt satisfied. The whole confusion that constituted reality now made sense. Everything was perfectly clear. All that seeking and questioning that had troubled his life was no longer. He'd received the answer. It was so simple he almost laughed. The meaning of life was clear. He knew his purpose now, and it was such a relief. His purpose on this planet was to serve the goddess Fiana in whatever capacity she required. And he did it gladly, basking in the feeling of freedom and peace and understanding. Simply basking in the now. It was as if enlightenment had come to him, and it was so simple, so perfect. Perfectly perfect. All that mattered was this moment, for this moment is all there ever was. And whatever she wanted in this moment, he would do. Forever.

Right now, his job was to guard the front door. Since he was, in fact, guarding the front door, he was happy. He did what she wanted. It was his purpose.

A group of people approached. He knew exactly what to do. No question. No doubt. He had been told, so it was clear. Everything was clear now.

These people looked uneasy, but they would not be for long. Confusion and doubt still plagued them, but not for long. Soon it would be good for them, too, and that made him happy. They had not yet received Fiana's blessing, and that's why they seemed so troubled. But not for long. That would soon be remedied. They would be healed, and they, too, will share in her glory. And it was good. It was all good.

He saw by the packs they carried that, like him, they had traveled far in search of understanding. He welcomed them. They would be his brothers and sisters in this paradise. Such paradise. Everything was so clear.

"Good evening, friends," he greeted them, and his voice sounded calm and peaceful and perfect. It was all so very good. "Your journey is at an end. Inside these halls, you will find gorgeous peace and understanding. All that you have yearned for. Just a few more steps, and it will all be yours."

"Fat chance," muttered the dark haired girl. Her jet-black bangs hung in a radical straight line just above her big green eyes. Green eyes, like his mistress. She was so beautiful, his mistress. Everything was so good. So perfect. It was all perfect. Perfectly perfect.

"I understand your doubts, young girl. I, too, had doubts when I first arrived, but you will soon see the truth. And it is glorious. Please come with me and bask in her presence. You will know the meaning of euphoria. You will see heaven. I'll conduct you to the chamber of revelation, and you will be saved. It's all so perfect. Perfectly perfect. It's all so good." He turned, and pushing open a door, gestured for them to follow him.

CHAPTER TWENTY-THREE

"This is such a trap." Maddy walked beside Aidan as they followed the young man into the stone compound.

"Of course, but it gets us in the front door, and that's not nothing."

"So we just follow this guy in, do we? Just walk right into her sadistic clutches? I'm not liking this plan anymore."

Rowan, just behind her answered. "The truce is in effect. She cannot harm us without breaking it. At least not until the sun rises tomorrow, and by then, her power will be dwindling."

"That doesn't mean she won't. Hello. Psychopath."

"That will be to our advantage."

"If we survive it. You've lived, like, forever. I'm just thirteen."

"Come on," said Aidan and followed the unwashed hipster through a wide hallway carved into the rock. It led into a vast chamber dominated by a statue rising from a fountain.

And they weren't alone there.

"Oh yeah. Trap."

Several score people stood around the walls wearing acolyte robes and holding staffs in one hand: an gaggle of wannabe wizards.

"Nice rod, Gandalf," Maddy said to one as they passed.

"Shhhhh!" Aidan chided. "Those could be used as weapons, you know. Let's not give them a reason, okay?"

The young man leading them stopped and turned. "Wait here and I will inform her divine ladyship of your arrival."

He headed for a long, winding stone staircase on the other side of the room. The companions continued to follow him.

Everyone else in the room didn't budge, but remained still. Eyes forward. Unblinking. It was as if they were made of stone themselves. Just like the statues that lined the walls and the large one in the fountain.

"That must be the one Moody spoke of," Maddy whispered to Aidan.

"Shhh."

As the hippie started his ascent, he noticed they hadn't obeyed his request. "Um. Didn't I ask you to stay by the fountain?"

"Yeah." Maddy said. "What of it? You're not the boss of us."

"But. Those are the rules. You must follow the rules. It's her will, and only when we follow her will are we at peace. No! Go back to the fountain!" The bland bliss on his face melted into a twisted scowl of confusion. "No! The doubt! You can't come up here yet! You must wait by the fountain until her divine ladyship comes to you! It's her will!"

"Is that so?" Aidan stepped up with Maddy. Both had their arms crossed in defiance.

"Yes, of course. It is good. It was good. I can only be good with her will. Follow her will!"

"And if we choose not to? What then, hippie boy?"

Every wannabe wizard with a staff moved in unison. Their stance now ready for attack, Gandalf staffs out in front.

"I am afraid we must insist." His face had returned to one of calm. Smooth. "It's all perfect. Perfectly perfect. As it should be. Her will. We just follow her will."

"I see." Maddy turned to Ms. McFey. "What is the moral prerogative here? I mean these people are not vampires, or even necessarily evil. They're just under a spell, nothing more than mental slaves really. Would it be right to hurt them?"

"Not if we can avoid it."

"But can we? I mean, if we have to. They intend to prevent us from rescuing our friends. Well, our friend, and then Trudy and Rex, too."

"There are too many of them, Maddy. What can we do?"

"They are also standing in the way of our escape! Anyone notice that?"

The hippie boy door guard rejoined the conversation. "There has been a misunderstanding. Clearly. We have already been set free. The words of the divine lady have freed us from doubts and uncertainty. From all pain and suffering. Everything is perfect. Please be patient just a little while and she will be here to free you as well. It's all so good."

"No thanks. We already know how she likes to free people. Not fun."

The hippie boy twitched again. "No. Disobeying is not possible. Control. Under her control. Always."

"Okay." Max did her best to answer Maddy's question. "I think, for all our sakes, that we should refrain from hurting anyone who is not manifestly an evil, undead creature. We should, in fact, do our best to delay a physical confrontation as long as possible."

"What do you think this whole conversation is about?" Aidan said. "If I were less scrupulous all these good people would be slowly roasting by now. But it's not their fault. They're the victims here. We're all in danger here, and we're wasting our time."

"No! Obey her!" the hippie boy said and grabbed Aidan's arm.

Aidan's arm glowed bright and hot. He howled in pain and leapt away, holding his hand close to his chest.

Fiana's other minions moved in, holding their staves in quite the threatening manner now. They moved as if they were all one. In unison. Step. By. Step.

Aidan continued to glow, so her friends moved away from her.

Rowan began chanting a protective spell, motioning the others with his arms to gather around him. The temperature around him dropped and then suddenly rose as Aidan burst into flame, driving back the minions who had been advancing on them. She walked towards them, flame pushing them away from the inner doors towards the hallway. They hissed and poked towards her with their staffs, but they kept moving back.

Her companions huddled against the wall behind Rowan's protective spell as she passed. When all the minions had been driven out of the room, she slammed and barred the door, leaving smoldering hand prints where she touched the wood. Once the doors were secure, her flame went out and she slumped to the floor. Her friends rushed over to her.

"What's wrong?" demanded Ms. McFey.

Aidan smiled weakly. "Doing that burns a lot of calories. And twice in such a short time. I'm starving. And a little woozy. Do I smell food?"

"The feast," Rowan said. "They're having a feast up these stairs. Follow me."

But before they could get far, the doors burst open. The bar with which Aidan had secured the doors just a few moments earlier slid from its sockets on its own accord, allowing the massive double doors to swing back open. They were again exposed to a disgruntled mob of minions.

"Go!" Max said to Rowan, and he sprinted up the stairs towards the high double doors at the top, behind which Rowan could sense the ambient power.

The others prepared to face the crowd of staff wielding acolytes with a weakened, hungry fire elemental.

"Um, too bad we're prepared to fight vampires," Maddy said holding her useless super soaker before her. "Yeah. I vote we go with Rowan."

"Agreed," Aidan said.

"At least halfway up," Ralph said. "That way they have to come up the stairs. Hopefully, the five of us can fight off one or two at a time. They are moving quite slowly, like they're hypnotized, huh?"

"Ya think?"

"Maybe they don't like water as much as they don't like fire," Ralph said. They all stood with their super-soakers, waiting for the advancing wizard wannabes to reach and ascend the stairs.

James shot an uncertain glance towards Fiana. Although completely bored, she mustered her dignity and tried to play the host. They all sat around a long, wooden table full of succulent food. This aspect of the ancient tradition she had not anticipated. Too many centuries had passed since anyone had dared. Still, tradition contained its own power. She would play this little charade out.

"So. Here is your blasted feast. Eat up and let's get down to business. Are you seeking justice then?"

"Not I, my lady." As Moody spoke he grabbed a rather large watermelon. "Who am I to dare such a thing? But this dear lady does." He motioned to Trudy sitting beside him, chewing on a cob of corn. She looked up at them both, startled, eyes full of fear.

Just then, Rex strolled through the side door. "Something smells delicious!" Upon seeing his mother, he turned ghost white and took an involuntary step back. "Mom? What are you doing here?"

"I've come to take you home." Anger brought fire back into her eyes. She turned from Fiana, and railed at her son. "What were you thinking? Running away from home like that! Do you have any idea how worried I've been?"

"But Mom..."

"Don't but Mom me. Do you have any idea what I went through to find you? Do you know what freaks I had to ride with for nine hours? NINE HOURS, REX!"

"But I..."

"But nothing. You're a minor. By crossing a state line with an adult you have made her a kidnapper. Do you realize that?"

"But mom..."

Fiana followed this exchange with amusement. The entertainment value alone ameliorated the inconvenience. Still, it must be dealt with and soon in a way as to discourage further ridiculous outbursts like this one. She motioned to James who bent his head in front of hers to receive her murmured instructions.

"Send servants to secure and guard all the doors, especially the front gate," she whispered to him. "We must be prepared for an attack from my loving husband and his rascals. I'm rather surprised they're not here yet. I haven't felt Rowan for awhile now. He was coming closer, but then..." She didn't finish her thought, and James nodded in understanding. In another moment, he stepped out of the room through the side door to issue those orders.

"Enough," cried Fiana over the scolding mother. "I have heard enough to render judgment. The boy shall decide."

"You will render judgment?" Trudy was on a roll now. "This is *my* son."

Fiana ignored her. "Do you, who bear the name of royalty, wish to return to your former life in your mother's household? Or would you prefer to remain here with me, to be my paladin, and to serve me in our fight against evil?"

Rex gave his mother a brief, cool glance before turning back to Fiana. "I will serve you, my angel."

Trudy gasped and fell backward, grabbing at her broken heart.

"So shall it be. The verdict is given. Have you aught else to say Moody?"

Before Moody could speak, Trudy recovered and erupted into a rage the likes of which few have seen. "How could you?" she screamed at her son. "I have pampered you, cared for you. I've sacrificed my own life and happiness for you ungrateful little snot." She reared back and slapped him hard across the face. "Your father was right! That bastard was right! The only thing you understand is violence." She reached back again, gathering momentum, but Rex covered his face with his arms and got out of her reach as her hand flung forward a second time. Moody grabbed her around the waist as she reached toward Rex, still swinging. "This little rebellion of yours has gone on long enough. You're coming home right now, young man, so get your butt over here." She glared at her son from within Moody's embrace, struggling to get free.

"Silence!" Fiana lost all patience. With a violent wave of her hand, Trudy's tongue clove to the roof of her mouth and she could not speak. The woman clawed at her throat and screamed silent screams; agony and fear poured from her wide eyes.

"Judgment has already been rendered in accord with the ancient tradition. I do not wish to hear from you further. I want to know what the herder of cats has to say."

Moody placed Trudy back in her seat in front of her half-eaten corn. "I accept your judgment as given, and recognize the justice within it."

Tears streamed down Trudy's cheeks. Heartbroken. Betrayed. Lost. Confused.

Fiana laughed at her pain. She put her arm around Rex. "I see!" she said with delight. "I know what has happened. How simply delicious! Oh, yes! Agony with such scrumptious ecstasy is a rare treat! Oh, my! The last person in the world that you could count on has abandoned you. You have no one left. Your husband is gone for a classier woman, I understand. And now your son chose a better woman as well. Oh so much better than you could ever hope to be. So, you are left with no one. How perfectly delightful. And what of the group of freaks? Huh? Where are they? Surely they're coming to rescue you, no? As much as you despise them, they are your only hope."

With this Trudy knew despair—utter despair and fear. She no longer feared death, for nothing could ever be worse than this feeling. In that moment, Trudy knew hell.

Moody, however, interrupted and persevered without apparent concern, "There is still the matter of your husband. He wishes the return of his stolen property."

"And I am to take your word for it? If he wishes it, then let him come forth and demand it himself."

Through the double doors leading from the ante chamber Rowan strode into the throne room, clad in his blue jeans and a his green cotton t-shirt, now bone dry in the desert air.

"I do request it."

"Fool," she smirked. Then, to her guards. "Seize him."

They leapt to obey, grasping his arms tightly.

"Hi, honey! So nice to see you, my love. My all. Did you miss me so much that you walk so lightly into my power?" she mocked. "Nice shirt, by the way. Very butch."

Rowan gave no reply, standing complacent.

Moody replied for him. "Do you break the truce then?"

"What do I care for the old ways? Their time is over. I am the new way. My word is the new law. I am more powerful than you can ever imagine, Moody Moody Marlin. You foolish, pathetic man."

Moody nodded

"Then your power over me is ended." With a swiftness belying his girth, he pulled out his wand and spun around, sending a burst of raw magic through the open doors towards the giant statue below, straight into its blue glowing eyes. As it struck, the statue burst into a spray of stone shards.

Fiana leapt to her feet. "No!"

But she was too late. She ran past them all to watch her statue crumble to the ground below. Even as the rain of fragments clattered on the floor, her minions began to awake from her spell, shaking off the compulsion that had been held in place by the

statue. They looked around with fear, then anger: the two ingre-
dients which, when combined, brewed a deadly hatred.

Fiana, in the heart of her fortress, suddenly realized she was
surrounded by a host of enemies, and the power she took from
her minions quickly melted away. Even so, she could probably
slay them all, but with Moody and Rowan, and who knew who
else lurking about, she was too exposed. She needed to regroup
in a more secure location. Then, counterattack.

Rex came out by her side and James rejoined them. They
watched the minions below have free will once again.

"There she is!" one of them shouted. Hundreds of eyes looked
up at her, and then hundreds of shaking fists and shouts filled
the air.

"I'm not beaten yet," she said. "Follow me. Both of you.
To the aerie." She strode back through her throne room, holding her wand before her. She tried to throw a spell onto those
traitors as she passed through, but Moody blocked her. "Don't
think you've won. Oh, Moody, Moody, Moody Marlin, you
can't leave. And neither can you, my darling. We're miles from
anywhere, and I'll catch back up with you soon enough." She
disappeared through the side door with her two remaining followers. She held her wand in her hand as they made their way
upwards through the corridors and stairwells, just in case they
tried to follow. And, anyone before them foolish enough not to
flee would be blasted out of existence. There had been only one
such fool between the throne room and the high aerie.

She had made a mistake, a tactical error, but she had other
tricks up her sleeve. "They destroy one army? I'll make another.
A stronger one. I just need a little time to summon another one.
A secret one they'll never suspect.

"Secure the door," she barked as they entered the aerie.

James pushed the heavy door shut and slid an iron bolt into place.

Rex stood in confusion, dumbfounded at the turn events had taken. Everything was spinning out of control. "Is my mom okay?"

"What? Shut up, boy. Enough with your sentimental nonsense at the moment. Let me think. I can still set things right, and maybe have a little fun in the mean time. James, you know what to do."

"You planned for this?" Rex said. "You planned for failure?"

"Insolent boy! This is not failure, just a...snag. This chamber has long been prepared for what I will do now. Everything is in place. There's a very good reason I chose this location for my desert fortress. It's not failure, stupid boy. It's genius. It's lifetimes of knowledge. It's about being prepared for every outcome."

Rex scowled. "I'm not stupid. Look, I think I'm going to go with my mom."

"Nonsense! You're mine. You made your choice. No going back."

"I'm going with my mom, and you can't stop me."

Fiana saw that the boy struggled between anger and fear. He balled up his fists and twisted his face in an ugly grimace, but tears filled his eyes and his face turned bright red. With great condescension, she looked down on him, put her hands on both his shoulders, and stared into his eyes with the cold, detached stare of a predotor. "Let's not do that," she said in a very patronizing voice.

Tears spilled over Rex's lids, which made him even angrier than ever.

Fiana's countenance changed in the blink of an eye. She went from looking evil and acting cruel, to being the angel he loved.

Her face turned sweet and her eyes became bright. Rex saw the woman he adored and softened beneath her touch.

"Yes, let's not do that," he parroted. "My place is here with you, my sweet angel."

"That's better," she said, patting his cheek. "Do not fear my young paladin. The forces of evil have assailed our very temple, but only to their own ruin. They have brought the Day of Judgment upon themselves, sowing their own demise. Now the trumpets shall be blown, not-so-metaphorically speaking. With a whisper across the winds, the dead will rise from their graves. A host of the righteous shall sweep the wicked from the land."

Rex nodded as if he understood, the poor fool. Perhaps she should have him dressed in motley. That would be more appropriate. She must remember that for after she'd won. That would be quite entertaining, indeed.

Rex's eyes followed her gaze to a gigantic brass horn, a cross between a french horn and a sousaphone but with more twists and turns. If Rex stretched his arms all the way out, side-to-side, he wouldn't be able to reach the edges of its seven foot bell. It protruded out over the high terrace, surrounded by the night sky beyond the compound, and at the end of its brass intestines the mouthpiece rested on a wooden stand inside the wide window.

Fiana wet a single finger by sliding it in and out of pursed lips and held it steady in the night air. "Perfect," she said. "The wind is north-northwest. How apropos."

Laughter more insane than any Rex had ever heard in any movie or video game erupted from her wide-open mouth. She set her lips to the enormous horn's mouthpiece, and Rex covered his ears, waiting for the thundering sound sure to follow. But she did not blow the instrument. Instead, she whispered words in an ancient tongue. As they traveled through the brass labyrinth, her words swelled in power, vibrating the brass, echoing through the instrument. The subsequent buzzing sound hurt Rex's ears, so he covered them, awaiting the thunderous sound to erupt from the other end. But there was none. Out the brass bell came the harshest, yet somehow the most gentle whisper ever breathed.

The evening zephyrs seized the magical words and carried them across the desert plains.

Down below, the rest of the crew came storming into the feast room just as Fiana fled out the side door with Rex and James.

"Way to go, Moody!" Maddy stopped to catch her breath. "That was too close."

"Yeah. Great timing, Uncle Marlin," Aidan said. "Even from our defensive position, those hordes were about to overpower us. Thank you."

"Oh! My dear! It was my pleasure. Yes! My pleasure! Holy Mackrel-andy! I wish you could've seen the look on her face. Yes. That was quite satisfying, indeed. Have they all gone? Last I saw, they were pretty angry."

"They're angry all right," Ralph said. "Wouldn't you be? They had their minds controlled by a psychopath, and they were made to believe they liked it. Fed a fantasy and convinced it was reality. I see some serious therapy in their futures."

"What happened to them?"

"They were furious when they saw Fiana, and I thought we were going to be trampled, but after she fled, they just kinda lost interest. I mean, in Fiana. They turned to each other and started trying to find their loved ones. I'm sure they won't just let this drop, though. I know I wouldn't."

A roar came from below and the sound of things being smashed followed by cheers wafted up the stairs. Ms. MacFey closed the heavy doors.

"Or, maybe they are still mad."

"Okay! I'm pumped." Maddy did a little dance under the influence of her adrenaline. "Let's get her! Let's go, now! Chase her down while we've got her on the run. C'mon!"

"No." Aidan said. "We need to find Rowan's wand first. That's what we came here for, and that's the most important thing now. Once he has it back, he'll be more powerful and we'll be able to free Cullen. Then we'll kick some serious backside."

"All right, but how? Do you know where it is?"

April covered her ears as the sounds from below got louder and louder. Now, not only from the inner chamber, but also from the outside beneath the balcony. Chaos reigned. Hundreds of her former minions were fleeing in panic. To have had their very will taken from them, to not even be one's own person, had horrified her victims. Some reacted by fleeing, wanting only to get as far away from the thoughts and location of such molestations. Others reacted with overwhelming anger. Grabbing up their tools, or whatever came to hand, they began to smash everything that could be broken, and loot any portable wealth they could find.

"How will we get past that?" April shouted over the din. "They're turning into a rioting mob!"

"Okay, first of all, everybody stay together." Ms. MacFey put her arm through Ralph's and invited the others to come in close as well. "In a nice, tight group. I don't want anyone getting separated in this mad house."

"Uncle Marlin, do you have any idea where the wand is?" Aidan felt much more safe now that she was back with her uncle, but things weren't over yet.

"I'm afraid I do not, my dear."

"I suppose it was a long shot. How about you, Rowan, can you feel it calling to you or anything?"

Rowan closed his eyes. "I can sense its general direction, somewhere beneath us and deeper into the mountain."

"Okay, we'll head that way. Is everyone here? Hey, Trudy. Are you coming or what?"

Trudy motioned with large, angry gestures at her mouth. Tears streamed down her face. The most piteous sounds were gurgling up from her throat, but no words came out.

"What's wrong? Can't you speak?"

Trudy opened her mouth to show the others that her tongue had been fused to her upper palate. Its sides flapped as she tried to speak, making unintelligible sounds of anger.

"Oh my dear! Forgive me! I forgot in the chaos," Moody said, placing his wand on her lips and whispering an incantation.

"Oh! Thank you, Moody!" She stuck her tongue in and out to ensure she had control over it again. "I'm ready. That witch made a fool of me and turned my son against me. Oh, I'm ready all right. I'm not going to put up with this nonsense anymore. Let's send the vampire bitch straight back to hell."

"Excellent. Let's move out."

"But the mob," April said, hands still covering her ears. At times like these, it wasn't a benefit to have heightened senses.

"I'll take care of them." Moody swung his arm in a wide circular motion. A wispy purple smoke streamed out from the end of his wand and settled in a circle around the group, forming a protection around them all. As if on an escalator, they moved out of the throne room and down the stairs, while awakened converts fled past them as if they weren't even there. Sounds of shattering glass and splintering wood filled the air along with angry shouts of vengeance.

The small group made their way deeper into the fortress, passing the angry reconverted and others who were weeping, sitting curled, rocking back and forth. Maddy felt everything that she passed, albeit muted thanks to being shielded between Rowan and Moody.

Moody directed them back down to where he had come from the dungeons. They passed all the cells and came upon a corridor that intersected theirs. It looked exactly the same down both directions. Then, there was always the choice of continuing on ahead as well.

"Which way?"

"Forward." Rowan said with authority. "I can feel it stronger now. Just follow me." He led them down the passage until it came to more stairs.

Down.

Down.

Down.

Fiana's underground warren proved to be a confusing maze, but Rowan followed the call. "We're close now." Many times they came upon roving groups of former followers bent on revenge, looting, and general mayhem, but Moody's spell held true.

The bowels of the fortress were larger than any of them could imagine, so it took them longer than they had hoped to find what they were looking for. They heard yelling, and then a crash. Rounding a corner, they saw about a dozen people. Several of them held a sideboard with the legs broken off. Others held the legs as makeshift clubs. The ones with the sideboard were ramming it against a stout door at the corridor's end, while the others cheered them on.

"Excuse me," shouted Aidan. "We'll open that for you if you would all just stand back a moment." The crowd stopped what they were doing and turned to look at the newcomers. By speaking directly to them, she had broken Moody's spell. They could now see them, and the faces of these scavengers showed them to be in an ugly mood.

"And who the hell are you?" snarled a young man, hefting a chair leg in a threatening manner.

"Everyone just calm down now. We're on the same side." Maddy emanated waves of calm in their direction. "We're the ones who broke the spell you were under. Besides, you don't want to mess with us. If you thought Fiana was bad, we're the ones currently kicking her butt."

"So you say," said their apparent leader, stepping forward. This young man had the largest piece of table leg in his hand and a murderous look in his eyes. "And I say you're in league with her." He pointed his club at Trudy. "I recognize that one. We came in together, but she was too good to talk to the likes of me. She wasn't hypnotized. When the rest of us were sent away to be slaves, she stayed behind. The spell didn't affect her. Curious, no?"

Trudy protested. "I'm not in league with her! I was saved by my faith in Jesus."

The young man scoffed.

"And what do you know, Cuckoo Boy?"

Aidan threw up her hands between the two of them. "Enough of this! Time is wasting!" She put forth her hand and the wounded sideboard burst into flames. With cries of fear the marauders threw it to the ground, leaping back in fear.

"See! They are witches! They are working for her! Get them before they can cast more spells!" Spurred on by his cries, they rushed forward.

Moody stepped forward and pointed his wand.

"*Stadaim!*"

The attackers froze in place, unable to move. Several of them, caught in mid-stride, didn't have both feet under them, so they fell over when the spell took hold, tumbling to the ground, still as statues.

"That wasn't the most impressive piece of diplomacy I have ever witnessed," Ralph said.

"Maybe not, but that was the only way it was going to end well. We haven't the time. They'll be just fine. However, I would recommend haste at this point. I can't hold so many for very long." His arms trembled with the effort, his legs braced against the invisible weight.

"Right." Rowan moved towards the door: a modern, steel security door, locked and bolted. He laid his palm against the lock. "It's warded. I don't think I can break it without my wand."

"And my wand is rather busy at the moment."

"Let me try." Ralph pulled out one of his devices, a duplicate of the one Rex had stolen from him. He moved forward.

"Wait," cried Aidan. "Won't that—" but it was too late.

Ralph pushed the button, and the device cancelled Moody's spell and all other magic around. Cuckoo Boy recovered quickly and grabbed Aidan who instinctively burst into flame. He screamed with pain, letting go and jumping away.

This enraged the others. Yelling defiance, they threw whatever they held in their hands, mostly bits of broken furniture, at Aidan. She crouched down, protecting her head with her arms from the rain of broken wood. Even so, the falling heavy wood bruised and scratched her.

"Do something!" Maddy exclaimed at no one in particular.

"Turn that thing off, Ralph!" Moody shouted.

"Oh! Right!" He fumbled his fingers over the mechanism, but instead of flipping the power switch off, the thing slipped through his fingers and crashed to the floor.

"Quickly!"

Ralph scrambled, picked up the device, and flipped the switch.

Moody threw a spell at the angry mob. An explosion of fire followed by billowing smoke separated the two groups in the hallway. "Quick. Gather close." He waved his wand in the big circle around them again. Purple smoke descended over them and protected them from sight once again. "This time, don't say anything," Moody whispered. "Just wait."

The smoke cleared and the angry mob, coughing and sputtering, once again set to move forward and attack them.

"Hey," Cuckoo Boy said. "Where did they go?"

"They must've slipped past us," another said. "Come on. They couldn't have gotten far."

They rushed off in the opposite direction and after a few moments, they could no longer hear their cries of fury.

Rowan helped Aidan to her feet and inspected her wounds. He wiped off the blood and murmured a spell to ease her pain.

"Thank you."

Ms. McFey took a deep breath. "Well, that did the trick. Now, how about that door."

"Um. Sorry about that. I'll try again." Not having a vengeful mob to contend with simplified matters. "Okay. Problem."

"What now?"

"It did its job by breaking the wards, but as soon as it was switched off the wards reasserted themselves."

"Well, turn it back on, sir. Turn it back on! I shan't need to use magic until we're inside."

"That's the problem. It won't switch back on. It must've been damaged in the fall."

"Let me try," Moody tried every spell he had learned in his long, long life, but nothing worked. "She has this protected against all magic. I'm afraid canceling the magic is our only hope. Any chance of fixing that thing?"

"I can try, but I don't have many tools with me. I'm so sorry, Rowan."

"We must get past this door. That much is clear, but our available magic can't break the wards. We are amidst a magical impasse. This is a problem, but not an insurmountable one. Other ideas? What are our options?"

"Can you do anything?" Max asked Aidan.

"Like what? Melt through the steel door or surrounding stone. I don't have the energy for that, not after being injured. And I still haven't eaten, so I'm even weaker because of that. Even so, I couldn't do it at my best."

"Here," Maddy said, offering Aidan a snack bar from her backpack. "This will help some."

"Thanks."

"The walls, maybe that's it." Max turned to Moody and Rowan. "Are the walls warded?"

Rowan placed his hands upon the stone beside the door, and Moody placed his on the other side. "It doesn't seem to be. Can you shift these stones, Marlin?"

"I can certainly try. If you would all just step back, my dears." He touched the tip of his wand to the wall and leaned towards it. As his considerable weight shifted forward, so did the stones in the wall, falling away from him and tumbling into the chamber beyond.

They were in.

April and Maddy crouched behind Aidan, still munching on her granola bar, this one from April's pack, and they all watched as Rowan, ignoring all the mystical paraphernalia surrounding it, strode forward eagerly to retrieve his wand. "Wait!" Aidan said with a mouthful.

Rowan looked back at her just as he stepped over the chalked circle surrounding it. After a loud snap and a flash of flame, a sudden, dense smoke filled the room billowing out of the opening. The girls coughed, waving their hands in front of their faces. The smoke dissipated, leaving the room as it had been, only without any sign of Rowan.

"Where did he go?" Trudy said. "He was just there. How could he just disappear like that?"

"The wand is still there," Moody observed. "We're not thinking straight, friends. We're too tired, too hungry, and too rushed. Now Rowan is gone." He sunk to the ground, head in his hands. "It was a trap. When will I learn not to underestimate my lady? She thinks of everything."

"He might be okay." Max's eyes filled with tears. "He has to be okay, right? I mean, maybe it just transported him into a cell or something. She doesn't want him dead, right? So he's probably okay. We just need to find him."

"How could he just disappear like that?" Trudy repeated.

"Maybe it's booby trapped just for him. What if I got it?" Aidan stood up with the help of Maddy and April. "I got it, girls. Thank you. Much stronger now." She moved toward the opening and started to step inside.

"Wait!" Ralph grabbed her arm. "Whatever happened may still be active. Let me go first. I should be able to defuse it. I think I got this thing working again. It was just a wire that had worked loose, so it should work again." He held up the device still in his hand and stepped through the opening, but just as he reached the chalk circle, electrical static discharged, throwing him to the floor.

"Ralph!" Max darted towards the opening, but Aidan's grabbed her before she, too, suffered Ralph's fate.

"No, Ms. MacFey. We can't lose another one of us."

Ralph groaned, letting them know that he still lived. He pushed himself up into a kneeling position, shaking his head. Straightening his glasses back onto his nose, he looked up to see all his friends huddled around the opening with worried expressions. "Hi!" he said.

"Are you all right?" The fear made Max's voice tremble.

"Yes, just a little shaken up." He staggered to his feet. "Don't come in until we figure out what other traps she's set." He wobbled over to where his device lay. The shock had thrown it from his hand. He picked it up, grimacing. "Now it's really ruined. Not just a loose wire this time." He pulled the cell phone out of his pocket. "This too. Fried. Totally fried." He threw them both down with self-deprecating force and shook his head in disgust. "I'm such an idiot."

"Nonsense. Could an idiot create all that you have? You have saved us more than once. Fiana is just stepping up her game. You couldn't have known."

"Would anyone other than a fool follow someone into a trap?"

"Don't be so hard on yourself. Rowan sprang the trap. How were you to know there was a second one?"

"Even so." He looked back through the opening. "Did Rowan have a phone?"

"No. He said he wouldn't know what to do with it, so he left it in the van."

Ralph nodded. "That makes sense then. Fiana must have trapped the room to destroy any electronics passing through. It's just bad luck that the one carrying the most was the one to set it off."

"Help me! There's something wrong with April." They all turned to see Maddy kneeling beside April's prone body.

"Oh no!" Max rushed to Maddy's side. "What happened?"

"I don't know. After the blast I looked around, and she was like this. Will she be okay? Please tell me she'll be okay!"

"Take off her goggles." Ralph kneeled beside April while Trudy, Rowan, and Moody kept their distance so as not to overcrowd her in the narrow hallway. "She probably received some feedback from the discharge. Check her pulse." Maddy whipped the goggles off her head and put two fingers on her wrist. Maddy had a long habit of checking her own pulse just to lament that she was still alive, so she found April's pulse easily.

"It's steady."

Everyone breathed a sigh of relief.

A low moan escaped April's lips as she regained consciousness.

"Fiana has anticipated every move we've made." Aidan was losing her confidence in leading. "Are we that predictable?"

Moody patted her on the shoulder. "Fiana has sprung some nasty surprises on us, my dear. But remember, we have sprung some on her as well. Don't lose heart! These traps were set to counter the abilities we demonstrated the last time we challenged her. We must remember that she knows what we can do and will have accounted for that in her defenses."

"What now then?"

"We came here for Rowan's wand, and while Rowan may be missing, we must believe the wand is within our grasp. We simply must find the courage to reach forth and take it."

Now that she knew April was okay, Aidan smiled her gratitude at his reassuring words. He was right, they were far from beaten. She went back into the room of traps where now Ralph stood studying the chalked circles and mystic runes around Rowan's wand.

"Here, catch." When Ralph turned to look at her, she tossed him her super-soaker. He caught it, but looked confused. "Use it to wash away the chalk lines." He nodded his understanding and began to circle the circle, spraying it down with the squirt gun as he did so. The chalk line dissolved into amorphous puddles.

By the time he had gotten all the way around, April felt better and had sat up. Ralph pulled a hoodie out of his pack and used it to start mopping away what was left of the chalk.

"Here goes nothing." Ralph inched forward one toe at a time until he had crossed where the chalk line had been. and picked up Rowan's wand from its resting place. Tucking it into his belt, he walked back through the doorway without suffering any more surprises. Everyone breathed a sigh of relief.

"What's happening?" asked April, who could no longer see the events happening around her.

"We got the wand," said Maddy.

"Where to now?" asked Aidan.

"I don't know," replied April. My visions haven't returned yet."

"We need to find out where Rowan is," declared Max. "Don't forget that wherever he is, Cullen is also."

Aidan agreed. "These are our goals as I see it: first, we must rescue Rowan..."

"And Rex," interrupted Trudy to show she was paying attention and would not be sidelined.

"...and Rex," affirmed Aidan. "Once we get the wand back to Rowan we will be in a more powerful position. Also, Cullen won't be trapped anymore."

"Are you still pretending that Cullen is somehow inside Rowan? Please. This is no time for make-believe, kids. This is serious. My son is in danger!"

"Look lady," Maddy started, but Aidan stopped her with a gentle hand on her shoulder.

"We are not pretending, Ms. Samuels. I know this is all difficult for you to take in so quickly, but we are not pretending. We've gone over this again and again. Just look at what you've seen tonight. You've seen me burst into flame and melt stone. You've seen magical barriers and more."

Max stepped in when she saw Trudy's face becoming flush with anger. "She's right, Trudy. This isn't the time. We may not all like each other or see eye-to-eye, but we are all on the same side."

"At least for now," added Maddy who reverted back into silence with a glare from Max.

Aidan rolled her eyes. "Finally, we need to get everyone out of here safely. If, during all this, Fiana and/or James happen to get destroyed, all the better! Is everyone with me on this?"

No one objected.

Rowan, meanwhile, appeared in Fiana's high chamber. She turned from the window as he materialized within the appointed circle. Teleportation traps could be tricky, as the alignment of the terminus took perfect precision, or else the traveler could end up anywhere, and the trigger had to be tripped at the right moment by the right person. Fiana, in her long life, had mastered the delicate balance required to pull it off flawlessly.

"Welcome, my love. I see you and your little friends made it further than I anticipated." She favored him with a malevolent smile. "Although, you see I was prepared for that as well. I hope you don't find the accommodations too restricting. I'm afraid you will be there for quite some time."

Rowan sized up his predicament with apparent calm. A small chalk circle about six feet in diameter surrounded him. He didn't need to move to know he wouldn't be able to leave the circle. Its power emanated from its invisible wall and filling the air with magic.

"I traveled extensively in the East during my long years of searching. And as you can see, I didn't waste my time completely. Studied hard and learned quite a few new tricks, like the circles of summoning and binding. How do you like it? I did quite well, don't you think?"

"I find it rather constricting."

Fiana laughed delightedly. "As well you should my pet. As well you should. But look"—she pointed out the window— "darkness comes. And with it, my real army will emerge. Those others that were so rudely dismissed from my service were but household servants and slaves to work my fields compared to what will come. Even now my true soldiers wake from their long sleep and claw their way to the surface."

Rowan gimaced, appalled by this pronouncement. "Did you truly dare to summon the dead? Have you no bounds? No soul?"

Fiana laughed again.

"That, at least, disturbs your calm. Even after all these years, you can still delight me."

Her smile touched Rowan's soul, remembering the way it was with her, how happy they had been. His heart ached at the memory, but this was not his wife. She had proved that again and again. This monster looked like his beloved, but the sweet smile was but a mask to hide the ugliness within. "You no longer practice any of the healing magics of life, woman. Now you have sunk to the depths of the foulest necromancies. There is a cost for such black magic. Surely you remember that."

"The cost will be paid by your friends and anyone who dares cross me."

"I fear more for you than for anyone else. It is a foolish thing you have done, and you will suffer for it." Rowan sensed the wrongness that crawled its way towards them, and it made his gorge rise.

His pity irritated her. "It is not I who is the fool, *sweetheart*. Nor will it be I who does the suffering." She turned to the window to watch for her coming army, lamenting that she took such little joy from his defiance. Perhaps deep inside she knew she had gone too far, but she was justified in this. Indeed. She had eternal life, after all. What did she fear? Just the gnawing hunger and overwhelming hatred bubbling up inside.

She hungered for life, true life. Only blood satiated her, but it never lasted for long. As the decades passed, it satisfied her less and less.

Hate filled her up, and her hate knew no bounds. For what had love given her? Nothing. A life of agony and despair. All this introspection did nothing for her, and having Rowan so close, he who knew her better than anyone, made her remember who she was and see who she had become. She shoved that remorse back down deep into the black hole that threatened to consume her, not allowing her inner turmoil to surface for Rowan to see. There was no place for it here or now. She had come too far, suffered too much.

There was no turning back now. She caressed the side of the great horn, grateful for its power.

"Is that how you did it? A summoning horn?" Although he had never seen such a horn before, he recognized it from tales during his years of study. "The dead move slowly, Fiana. Just how much time do you think you have?"

"You underestimate me still, my love. Don't you know by now that I think of everything? This fortress is positioned near an old Native American battleground, so there are plenty of dead nearby. This is old magic."

"I am well aware of the magic necessary, and it is not one that ever works out well for the user. You know better."

"Oh, sweetheart. I do know better. I know better than you, and I certainly know better than Moody Moody Marlin. I am better. All those stories were about mere mortals, not a supernatural goddess. I'm unique, Rowan. I'm more than a witch now. More than a vampire, too. I am a goddess!"

"Your arrogance has triumphed over your good sense, woman." *And she has trapped me and Cullen in the center of it.*

Cullen heard his thoughts. "What am I in the middle of?"

"How dare you!" Fiana sneered, then turned to James. "Do you hear the insolence of this man?"

"I do, my lady."

"But insolence and bad manners will not stop me. Go down and take charge of our new army. Lead them through the palace and kill everyone who remains within. When the place has been sanitized, we will begin the great work. Take the boy with you. He looks rather bored. It will give him something to do."

James bowed and motioned Rex to follow him. Rex hefted his Rod of Righteousness and fell in beside James, his face marred with an evil grin of anticipation.

"Rowan!" Cullen shouted inside Rowan's head, causing Rowan to wince. "What is going on?"

Rowan couldn't do much in this predicament, but he could at least give Cullen an honest answer. *Fiana has attempted to raise an army of the dead. And by all indications, she has succeeded.*

"What! Can she do that?"

I'm afraid so.

"So not only do we have to deal with vampires, but zombies now too?"

That appears to be the situation.

"And not only have you lost your wand, trapping me inside, but now you're trapped as well."

That is also the case.

"What's the plan for getting out of this mess?"

As of yet, we have none.

"Well, we better get busy then."

I am open to suggestions.

"At the moment, the only thing that occurs to me is to wait to be rescued. But I think we need something a little more proactive."

I agree. But my activity is extremely limited in these magical confines. And yours, even more so.

"How about starting with breaking this spell then. What do you know about it?"

Very little, I fear. It is not a technique I am familiar with. The energy bonds are very strange. If I had my wand, I might be able to do something, but even then, it would be doubtful.

"Then I guess we're stuck with waiting to be rescued."

Seemingly so. But we can use our minds to search for alternate solutions while we wait.

"Yeah, I guess so. But she just sent James down to kill everyone. That does not sound good for our friends or our rescue," worried Cullen.

They are in a better position to deal with them than we are, Rowan replied. *Have faith. They'll find a way.*

CHAPTER TWENTY-FOUR

The desert winds Fiana had summoned blew across he burial grounds, blowing away the surface sands. They entwined into swirling tangles, propelling each other into a vortex that gravitated to and danced upon the graves. Increasing their velocity, they became spinning whirlwinds that threw off the soil with growing force. From beneath, mummified hands and skeletal fingers clawed their way upwards. The dead rose.

But these were not rotten corpses. Decomposition required moisture. The desert had dessicated the dead before decomposition could begin, mummifying the remains and leaving them whole save for the water content they had possessed in life.

When they reached the surface, the winds changed once again. Gathering together into a single force, it blew towards Fiana's keep, driving the shuffling mob towards it.

Tattered strands of fine suits hung from the leathery remains of former mobsters with names like Bugsy and Tiny who had come to the desert to create a recreational paradise; only the men in these forgotten graves had made some grave mistake themselves and just disappeared.

Even older corpses, natives from over a century ago, with feathers dangling from the brittle strands of dark hair emerged.

Once black tattoos covered their flesh as symbols of their totem, but now their shriveled arms showed ink faded to a dull grey.

These and more had been called from their long sleep to serve, and serve they would.

Rowan's words proved prophetic. April still hadn't recovered enough to try locating Rowan, so they backtracked to the throne room. Once there they rested until they figured out what to do next.

But next happened to them first. James came strolling in, with Rex at his heels, as if they still owned the place. They may have thought they did, since all the cultists had fled, but they seemed surprised to find the invaders camped out in their main hall, blocking their way to the entrance. They stopped, looking around apprehensively.

Trudy jumped to her feet. "Rex! Thank God I found you again. We've got to get out of here. These people are crazy!"

"Leave me alone. I told you, I'm staying with my angel."

"No you're not, young man. Get over here. We're leaving right now."

"But, Mom, it's the apocalypse, and I wanna fight against evil and wickedness."

"The what? Have you lost your mind?"

"It's true. I've joined forces with the Lord."

Maddy snorted derisively at this pronouncement.

Rex and Trudy ignored her.

"This isn't the apocalypse, and these people have nothing to do with the Lord. That man's a vampire for Christ's sake. Can't you see he's got a knife sticking out of his chest?"

"He's a martyr. He suffered in Jesus's name and been granted eternal life because of his faith."

"Are you on drugs? Stop this nonsense and get over here right now. We are going home."

"Go home then. I don't need you to rescue me. I'm old enough to take care of myself."

"I am not leaving without you."

"Well, I'm not going. I'm staying with my angel. She is the truth and the light."

With desperation in her eyes, Trudy appealed to Moody, who stood with his wand in his hand. He ignored her pleading look and kept his eyes on James, for he was a far more dangerous and immediate threat than problems between a mother and son. He could kill them all in the blink of an eye. So Moody didn't blink.

James had eased himself back towards the hallway. Although he was powerful, he knew the odds were against him when faced with Moody's skill. While everyone else's attention was focused on the argument between Trudy and Rex, James took the opportunity to maneuver himself near an exit.

Moody began to raise his wand.

James placed a hand on Rex's shoulder and yanked him back into the passage way.

Trudy leapt after them, but Max grabbed her arm and held her back. "Wait. You have no idea what he's capable of."

"He has my son!" Trudy tried to pull away, then noticed how white Max had turned. Her entire body trembled in fear. "Your neck," Trudy said, removing Max's hand from where it had instinctually had gone. "Did he do that?"

"He did."

Trudy nodded and understood. She knew abuse and the horrific aftereffects. "This is serious, isn't it? I mean, he could kill us. He could kill Rex."

"Yes. He could. In an instant. But he won't hurt Rex, I don't think. Fiana still needs him. We, on the other hand..."

April screamed, "They're coming in the front door."

Aidan spun around. She could see nothing. She turned a questioning glance towards April, only to see her crouched over and holding her head.

"What is it? What's coming?"

"Zombies. The dead have risen and are marching upon the building." In the silence following her revelation, everyone listened to the almost-inaudible rustling noise coming from the darkened fountain chamber. Hordes of shambling zombies had made their way into the palace.

"What do we do?" Aidan asked Moody.

"Leave the immediate area as quickly as possible."

"All right, let's follow those two. They may be heading back to Fiana. With any luck, Rowan won't be far from her. Everyone follow Moody. I'll play rear guard."

"As you wish, my dear." Moody moved swiftly to follow James and Rex. The others followed close behind.

Aidan waited to see what would come through the doorway, and she didn't have to wait long.

A walking corpse stumbled through, but like none she had ever seen in a zombie movie. This corpse had been drained of all moisture by the desert, a walking mummy. Only instead of bandage, scraps of animal skins hung from its emaciated loins. Its mouth contorted in a silent scream, and its vacant eye sockets gaped, threatening to consume her into the depths of death.

She suppressed a shudder and concentrated, sending a ball of flame directly into its chest. It hovered inside where its heart used to be, but it still staggered towards her. Aidan focused her energy on the fire and willed it to spread. The smell of burning leather filled the air, and Aidan covered her nose and mouth, protecting herself from the stench.

The doorway was now filled with teetering death, eerily silent. No sounds came from their empty throats, just a dull shuffling from where their feet slid across the floor. The fire ball had grown and it crackled as it ate the gnarled flesh.

More zombies piled through the door, and in a moment, she would be taken over by them. If they bit her, would she become a zombie like in the movies? Aidan didn't want to stick around to find out. She took a deep breath, gagging as the fetor filled her nostrils and her lungs, and with all the strength she could muster, she pushed her will into that ball of flame.

It burst into a conflagration consuming that zombie and spread rapidly to the corpses crowding up behind it. As their legs burned, they fell on top of one another, piling up in the doorway and creating a blockade. By the fire's light, she could see a horde of walking corpses filling the fountain room and beyond, as far as the light extended. She would not be able to burn them all and have any energy left for her own escape.

"That should at least slow them down," Aidan turned away from the horrific sight and hurried after her friends, slipping as she reached the stairs. That had taken a lot out of her, and she needed some food and quick.

Aidan caught up with her friends as they gathered around a locked door blocking further progress. "What's the holdup?"

"Maddy stated the obvious. "The door's locked."

"Well, get it open. There are about a million zombies who will be here any moment. If we don't get through that door, we'll be trapped here. I've slowed them down, but–" Aidan bent over and put her hands on her knees to catch her breath.

"Got another power bar?" Maddy asked April.

"Yes. In my backback."

Maddy found April's last granola bar and unwrapped it for Aidan.

"Thank you," Aidan said, then bit into the bar. "Moody, can't you do something?"

"At the moment, I am powerless my dear. Someone is standing on the other side of this door with an activated power disruption device."

"Great, now what?" Aidan studied the solid steel door. No way she could burn through it, or break it down for that matter. "I don't suppose any of you can pick a lock?"

"Why are you looking at me?" demanded Maddy.

"All right, then. It looks like we're going to have to fight our way out of here. Let's get as far away from this door as we can before that happens. I would feel much better facing a horde of zombies if Moody could use his wand."

Everyone nodded their agreement except Trudy, who seemed reluctant to abandon the pursuit of her son. She followed along with them anyway, not wanting to be left on her own.

The throne room was half filled with the shambling dead by the time they got back. Her fire had burned itself out, leaving behind a pile of half burned corpses still squirming and crawling with whatever body parts remained intact on top of a pile of ashes. More filed in from the outer hall, now with unimpeded access. The adjacent room contained even more, pushing their way forward.

Aidan made a quick decision. "There's no way we're going to get through all of them. Head for the only clear passageway," she said, pointing. "We'll try to find another way out, or up." She cast some fire at the zombies as the others made for the passage.

The desiccated corpses burned better this time, having more wicking in the form of tattered clothing, but they also burned hot. The temperature rose quickly, turning the un-vented room into an oven.

She refrained from lighting any more fires. The heat did not bother her, but she didn't want to roast everyone else. She ran into the passageway after the others.

Moody had waited for her.

"Thank you, Uncle."

"That's my girl. Nice work," he said. "Let me help." He used his wand to place an invisible barrier over the entrance. "That should slow them down for a bit."

They caught up with the others, who waited for them at the first intersection.

"Which way now?" Ralph asked.

Aidan turned to April, who held tightly to Maddy's hand. "How's the head?"

"Migraine, but functional. I can see openness to the right."

"We'll go that way then. Follow me."

The way lacked lighting, so they all took out their flashlights. Max passed April a couple of ibuprofen tablets. "Take these, and drink plenty of water. It will help with the headache."

"Thanks." April smiled her gratitude.

Aidan led them down the dark corridor, wondering if they would ever find Rowan again and get out of this cavern palace. That fear, at least, soon showed signs of being groundless. An opening to their right revealed ascending stairs.

"Is this the way?" she asked April. "I'm so turned around after all the back and forth. Does this feel like the way?"

"Yes," April said. "Keep going. It leads to the light."

"Fresh air!" Maddy said. "What are we waiting for?"

Smoke from burning corpses had followed them down the corridor, and ascended the stairs with them. They choked and gagged, each covering their mouths and guiding themselves along the stone walls. They all could have done without the stench, but the smoke also held a promise. This kind of convection indicated an opening to the outside world somewhere above them. It led them to an entrance on the cliff face.

They hit a landing first. The stairs continued up to a second landing and a third staircase that brought them to a luxuriantly furnished drawing room. Moonlight filled the room, so they switched off their flashlights to save the batteries and hide their presence. Moody closed the door behind them and sealed it with a spell.

French doors stood open the the night sky beyond. Their glass panes lay scattered in shards around them. Vengeful cultists had obviously paid this room a visit. They moved past the disarray onto the balcony. A low stone wall surrounded it, keeping them from tumbling over the edge to the canyon floor beyond. A broken end table lay against it, obviously thrown through the glass doors, shattering them in the process.

Moody placed a finger against his lips, warning them all to be quiet. They peered over the edge. There was nothing between them and a courtyard full of zombies three stories below.

Aidan looked up. The end of a giant brass horn protruded from a terrace one story up and some ways to her left. The indistinct murmur of voices drifted down to her from within it. She couldn't understand any of the words, but she recognized Fiana's voice. She still heard it in her nightmares.

Turning back to the others, she pointing up to that terrace, and they all nodded to show they understood. Now they knew where Fiana was, and likely where Rowan was, but they didn't know how to get to her yet.

Aidan strained her ears, but couldn't make out any of the conversation. Giving up she motioned everyone to follow her back inside, where they could have a whispered conversation without being overheard.

"We need to find out what Fiana's up to," she whispered. "I can't hear what they're saying. Does anyone have any ideas? Can you hear them, April?"

"Just voices, but it's still too soft to make out any words. I can try for a vision. I should be able to manage that."

"Okay then, see what you can do."

Maddy led April to an undamaged chair and sat her down, kneeling beside her and keeping hold of her hand. April bowed her head and remained still for some moments. Everyone else stood gathered around her, watching silently.

She began to speak. "She's up there. In a room much like this one, only with less broken furniture. She's talking to James. I don't know what they're saying. Rowan is there, too, standing in the corner, not moving. There's a small circle chalked on the floor around him. It's giving me a funny feeling."

"Is Rex there?" asked Trudy.

"No. No one else is in the room."

"He's probably the one using the disruption device on the other side of that door we couldn't get through." Ralph guessed.

"You're probably right," acknowledged Aidan.

April lifted her head, signaling that the vision had ended.

"Now what?" asked Maddy.

Aidan considered for a moment. "We figure out how to get up to that high chamber. Surprise them from behind. Take out Fiana and James, rescue Rowan, and give him his wand back. Then, we go down and grab Rex, relieve him of his device and bat, and head for home."

"What about the zombies?" asked Ralph. "We can't just leave them wandering about."

"If we can do something about them, we will. But they are secondary at this point."

"I should be able to do something about that," Moody offered, "and Fiana, too. If I can get a few moments with that horn up there."

"Why? What's the horn for."

"It is what she used to summon the dead."

"Okay then," agreed Aidan. "First we need to figure out how to get up to that room."

"I brought this." Ralph pulled out a coil of rope.

"That's great," said Maddy. "How many of us do you think can pull ourselves up that?"

Ralph looked towards their destination. "Probably none of us," he admitted. "Other suggestions?"

"How about having Moody levitate us all up to the terrace?" Maddy had quite the imagination.

Aidan turned to Moody. "How about it?"

"It could be done. Yes, indeed. But only one at a time, and I would not be able to levitate myself. I'm afraid Newton would have something to say about that, equal and opposite you know."

"Who's Newton? And what does he have to do with any of this?" asked Maddy.

Ralph sighed. "Laws of motion, Sir Isaac Newton. When he lifts something, even by magic, the weight of that object is transferred through his body to the ground. He can't do that if he's lifting himself."

"All right." Aidan juggled the possibilities in her mind. "How about this..."

CHAPTER TWENTY-FIVE

The top of the cliff was only about forty feet above their balcony, just twenty above Fiana's window. Ralph went up first, bringing his rope with him. Despite the danger, he rather enjoyed the experience. Being floated into the night sky by ancient faerie magic had a certain charm to it. His landing proved a bit bumpy, but Moody had warned him that it would be. Once over the lip of the cliff, he went beyond Moody's line of sight, so Moody just dropped him from about a foot off the ground. As soon as Ralph recovered his balance, he peeked over the edge and waved to Moody below.

Max came up next. Ralph caught her as she came within reach, easing her landing. And who was there to blame them if they clung to each other longer than necessary?

When they parted, Max took over air traffic control duties for the three girls while Ralph secured one end of his rope around a boulder heavy enough to take even Moody's great weight. To the astonishment of everyone, Moody confidently declared that he could mount the rope under his own power. They took him at his word, assuming that he possessed supernatural fey strength, which indeed proved to be the case.

Trudy stayed behind, because, as she declared, "I am not going to be wafted into the sky over a canyon filled with zombies. I will stay right here, thank you very much. When you've finished your business, you can just pop around the normal way and open the door for me."

No one argued with her. Although no one said it, they all felt rather relieved at not having her around while they confronted Fiana in her high chamber.

Once Moody finished his climb and joined the others, they all moved quietly over to a position just above Fiana's chamber window. Ralph retied the rope so it would fall just onto the terrace next to the giant horn.

Twenty feet below, four people, inhabiting a total of three bodies, continued their various activities, or inactivity, as the case might be, ignorant of what went on outside their room.

"Maybe you could rub away the circle with your foot," suggested Cullen.

The circle cannot be affected from the inside.

"You could try spitting on it. That may wash away enough to neutralize it."

It would still be coming from inside, so would not damage it.

Their mental conversation was interrupted by James: "My lady, the others have survived the room of traps. They set upon me in the throne room. I could not get past them. I locked the lower door and left Rex standing behind it with the device to prevent them opening it by magic."

Fiana nodded. "Their survival was not unexpected. Our army of dead will have entered by now and have them trapped. Soon they will all be dead. We'll wait here and let our army do its work. Afterward, we'll go and retrieve the wand from below, then we can proceed with my husband's conversion."

James bowed to her. "As you wish, my lady, so shall it be done."

Cullen gave a mental groan. Things just kept getting worse. "It sounds like we're not the only ones in need of rescue."

That seems to be the case. However, do not despair yet. Our friends are formidable and may come out of this yet. Fiana has grown too arrogant in her own power over the centuries. She has acquired the habit of underestimating her opponents.

"Still, we are the ones stuck in this circle, and our friends are about to be attacked by zombies."

That is also true. But all we can do is hope they triumph. I can see no way to help them, nor even ourselves. We must resign our will to the universe. There is nothing we can do.

Fiana took a seat facing the door. "Tell me James, do you think it would be worthwhile to rule this miserable little world?"

James looked confused at the question. "What do you mean, my lady?"

"Sometimes I wonder if it is worth the effort, all those petty mortals with their petty games and brief lifespans. I wonder sometimes if I should bother."

"It would provide some amusement."

"True, there is that. And existence does get rather tedious after the first few centuries. Soon, Rowan's power will be joined with my own. Finally, we will be one in flesh, taking him inside of me. Absorbing his power. Consuming his will. Devouring his soul. I will become the most powerful creature on this planet. I will be a deathless queen. All will bow down before me and worship me."

"So shall it be, my queen."

"Since the end is inevitable, it's best to accept it and proceed in the most efficient way possible. After all, there is more than one way to conquer a world."

"Indeed so, my lady."

James's role in the conversation was to listen and agree with everything Fiana said.

Cullen found this pathetic for both of them. They did not really interact. She reveled within her own ego, while he worshiped her without a will of his own.

They almost deserved each other.

"I don't like the idea of political power," Fiana continued. "It is too exposed, too prone to revolutions. One always has to deal with armies and wars. Military conquest can be great fun, but very inefficient. Really, too much effort. Easy, that's what I want. All the good, none of the bad. Genuine happiness, all the time. Religion. Yes. That's the way. I've acquired quite the taste for religion. That is rather easy with these vacant-minded sheep. I quite like the idea of becoming a goddess. What do you think? Would you like to be my high priest?"

James bowed to her. "I would be honored to serve in such a capacity."

Fiana laughed. "I'm sure you would. But tell me, my pet—" She broke off at his sudden look of astonishment, frowning.

He threw his arms in front of his face as his arms burst into flame.

Aidan swung through the open window on a rope.

Fiana whirled to face her, with a wand already in hand, but Aidan fell to her hands and knees as she landed. Fiana's spell flew harmlessly over her to shatter against the wall.

Before Fiana could ready another spell, Moody slid down the rope, landing with surprising agility on the window sill. She moved her wand to cover him, but his wand was quicker, and he managed to deflect her spell.

James cursed, beating at the flames covering his arms.

Something slid from Aidan's hand across the floor and into the circle, marring its outline as it did so. Rowan bent quickly and picked up his wand.

Relief flooded through Cullen. He could be free again, if they survived the next few moments.

Rowan easily dismissed what little power remained in the broken circle with a flick of his wrist and stepped from within its confines. He sent a stunning spell at his wife's back, but by some sixth sense, she anticipated this new threat. Whirling with inhuman speed, she managed to deflect it, giving Moody time to jump to the floor. He maintained his footing and his aim, which held steady on Fiana.

Nearly surrounded by enemies with more possibly on the way, Fiana retreated towards the door. She held her wand ready, trying to cover all three adversaries, not daring to cast a spell lest the other two pounce on her at that instant.

James tore off his jacket, leaving it smoldering on the floor. His arms were badly burned, but no longer on fire. No one was paying him any attention at the moment, so he ran to the door and yanked it open. He leapt through, followed closely by Fiana, who sent a blinding burst of light from her wand as she did so. James slammed the door shut in time to block the counter attacking spells, but there was no way to secure it from the outside.

"Come quickly," Rowan heard Fiana's cry through the door as he and the others blinked their vision back into working order. By the time they'd recovered, it was too late to follow. Fiana was probably even now letting her zombies through the lower door, and before long, they would be here.

Rowan locked the door into the room and placed a ward upon it. It might slow them down, but wouldn't hold them for long. He turned to Aidan. "Where are the others?"

"They're waiting on the cliff top."

"We should join them, quickly."

Aidan nodded. "Moody wants to try something with the horn first."

Rowan looked to Moody. "Are you sure you know what you're doing?"

"Indeed, better even than Fiana. She had contemplated this magic before, when I still gave her my loyalty. At that time, I had managed to dissuade her, but I took the precaution to learn all I could about it. The desert winds carried her command to raise the dead, so the power of that same zephyr will carry my words as well. If I don't do this, her words will wake the dead everywhere the wind takes them. And my words will break that unnatural spell."

Moody breathed the words into the horn, and they vibrated through the twists and turns, coming out the large end. The zephyr carried their power across the desert and around the world, ensuring all the dead rest in peace. Then he and Rowan stood together and with their combined magics shattered the horn into a billion brass shards. The blast threw Moody and Rowan backwards.

The earth itself trembled.

"No one will ever use it for such sacrilege again." Moody struggled to stand, but slipped and plopped down again.

Rowan reached out to Moody, but a ragged brass shard had embedded itself in his leg. He winced in pain, and Aidan ran over to him.

"You're hurt." She examined the wound.

"Not badly," he assured her.

"It looks bad enough. Hold still." She grabbed the shard, and got a firm grip on it, despite the slick blood covering it. Bracing her other hand against his leg, she yanked it out and tossed it aside. She slapped her hand over the wound as fresh blood began to flow. With a quick burst of hot fire down her arm and into her hand, she cauterized the wound.

Rowan gasped at the sudden pain, and Cullen screamed inside his head. "It's all right, Cullen. It's over. We will not be safe here long. After that explosion, Fiana will know exactly where we are. It will not take her long to break the holding spell I put on the door."

Moody made it to his feet on his own and stumbled over to the door. Placing his own wand on the lock, he sent a short burst of energy into it, fusing it into a solid lump.

"That should hold long enough for us to get out of here."

CHAPTER TWENTY-SIX

Rex grew bored with sitting in the semi darkness, guarding a locked door. This duty began with plenty of excitement, fleeing their enemies and slamming the door practically in their faces. That was fun. He heard what they said through the door, so he knew how well he'd foiled their plans with that anti-magic thingy. The Martyr had gone to tell Fiana what had happened, and told Rex to guard the door in his absence. The Martyr had said that Rex was their most important line of defense.

Rex felt proud of the responsibility entrusted to him.

But now he didn't know what to do. The freak squad had left, so did he still need to guard the door? No one came back. Neither the Martyr or his mom. Had they forgotten about him? Impossible. He was too important. He wielded the Rod of Righteousness and the anti-magic thingy, after all.

His faith was strong. They'd be back for him. This was just a test, that's all.

How had his mother found him anyway? Cullen's friends must have brought her, filled her head with lies and got her worrying. He wondered what to do about her. She obviously lacked the true faith despite her church-going. If she had kept the faith, then she wouldn't have failed her husband, forced him to find comfort elsewhere. She wouldn't have driven his father from their home. If she had only been pure and good like his sweet angel. None of this would be happening. It was her fault.

He heard shuffling noises from the other side of the door. Was someone still on the other side, hoping he would go away? Or was it just his imagination? Why didn't the Martyr come back?

Sounds of chaos from above jerked him from his musings. A fight had broken out. He wondered if he should go help, or maybe just have a look to make sure everything was okay.

A door slammed and rapid footsteps got louder, heading his way. He stood ready, with his Rod of Righteousness in his hand.

Fiana and the Martyr came rushing down the stairs. The Martyr looked in worse shape than before, with burned arms and a singed face. And the dagger was still sticking out of his chest. He'd lost his jacket and eyebrows as well.

Fiana appeared unhurt, but then she was an angel after all. She gave him a wry smile. "The wicked employed trickery and came at us from behind. They play dirty, as evil always does. You have kept a faithful watch down here; however, the enemy is now above. It is time to join our army, so that we may be victorious!"

Rex's ego swelled at her words. He had done his duty faithfully, despite the uncertainty and boredom. Now, he would lead an army of the risen to even greater glory. He had been chosen by God and his angel for this great task, and he would perform it with bravery. He tightened his grip on his Rod of Righteousness and followed his beautiful angel out the door into the hallway filled with slow-shuffling zombies.

Rex stepped in front of his angel, protecting her against the filth that filled the corridor. Using his Rod of Righteousness, he bashed an undead square between the eyes, cracking its skull. Another blow split it in two. But the thing kept moving.

"What are these things?"

"My army, sweetheart. Aren't they lovely?"

"Lovely? They're disgusting! Ugh! And that smell!"

"Ambrosia." Fiana said, wafting her hand in front of her nose, breathing in the horrid stench of death.

Rex kept hitting until the zombie was a pile of broken bones crumpled at his feet.

"That was quite entertaining, Rex. Bravo!"

"There are too many," Rex said, breathing hard. "I can't stop them all on my own."

"No need. They are under my control." With a wave of her hand they all stopped moving. "Make a path for us."

They obeyed.

"Now, follow us." Fiana filed through the zombie-lined corridor, strutting and swinging her bell sleeves to and fro. Flanked by her minions, she swelled with pride.

The zombies dropped. Inanimate. Dead again.

Fiana stopped so abruptly that Rex and James bumped into each other to avoid running into her.

"Get up," she said. "Stand up, you idiots." She kicked one, but it didn't move.

"The spell is broken," James said.

"Yes. Thank you, James. I can see that."

"How could that be?"

"Moody. It's that meddlesome melancholy man. He did this."

"Now what?" Rex said, shouldering his Rod.

"Plan C?" James offered.

"Don't be insolent, James. Do you need another reminder?" Fiana indicated the dagger.

"No, my lady."

"But there is another plan, right?" Rex said. "What's next?"

"Rex?" Trudy poked her head out of the room just down the hall. "Is that you?"

"Mom!"

"Ugh!" Trudy scowled at the piles of dead. "How horrid!"

"Move aside, woman," Fiana strode forward, pushing Trudy aside.

James followed.

Rex tried to join them, but Trudy grabbed him and hugged him tight. "Mom! Stop!"

"No! We're going to get out of here. Follow me. She's distracted and we can get away."

"No! I told you! I'm staying with my angel." Rex pushed out of her arms, throwing her to the ground.

"Rex!" Trudy grabbed at his feet, but he just kicked her in the stomach and yanked his foot away. He moved to join Fiana and James on the balcony, leaving Trudy crying on the floor, but he was stopped cold in the center of the room when Fiana let out the most terrifying cry of rage, cursing the heavens.

CHAPTER TWENTY-SEVEN

Moody levitated Aidan out and up to the cliff top where the others still waited.

Rowan soon followed. When he'd gotten his feet under him, he brought Moody up.

"What happened?" Maddy asked, while they were trying to catch their breath.

"Are you hurt?" asked Max.

Aidan answered. "Fiana and James are no doubt on our tail. We got Rowan, as you can see. He's hurt in the leg, but not bad. I tended to the cut" She peered over the edge of the cliff. "It looks like the zombies are all dead, properly dead I mean."

"Good," said Ralph, "because we need to get back to Trudy and get outta Dodge. But there are still a couple of vampires to worry about, one of whom is a very powerful witch. We don't have anything to neutralize her power with anymore."

Maddy wasn't sure she wanted to deal with Trudy again. "Can't we just leave her?"

"No," snapped Aidan. "Even if we don't like her, she is still part of this team."

A loud cry sounded from the room below.

"Was that Trudy?"

Maddy picked up a rock about the size of her head and peered over the cliff.

Aidan motioned everyone else to get moving. Just enough moonlight remained to reveal the rough outlines of the cliff down to where it met the canyon floor. She focused on the square of light spilling out onto the balcony below and saw Fiana and James step onto it.

James pushed Fiana out of the way and stepped aside himself, barely avoiding the rock Maddy had dropped with deadly aim.

"I bet they won't be coming out again any time soon, but"— she picked up another rock—"just in case." She poised the rock ready to drop as soon as someone peeked out.

Rowan had just begun to levitate Moody down when Fiana's wand suddenly darted out of the open doors and sent a burst of power up towards Maddy. Yelping, she leapt backwards, dropping her rock. The edge of the blast caught her a glancing blow, and she lost her balance. With a cry of despair, she fell off the cliff, desperately clawing for a handhold, but the cliff face lay beyond her reach. The ground rapidly approached, and she looked death in the face. In the seconds between the top of the cliff and the ground, everything moved in slow motion.

She saw the rock she dropped hit Fiana's hand, knocking her wand free.

She saw Moody, alerted by her outcry, catch her with his own magic, slowing her descent.

She saw Rowan's hold on Moody falter, thrown off balance because of Moody's attempt to save her, and she watched him tumble down towards her.

She struck the ground hard enough to drive the air from her lungs, but not hard enough to break any bones.

Moody made a similar landing several yards away.

Wild hope flared within her as she followed the wand's descent. It landed a few feet away.

Fiana raged and scorched the air above them with curses.

As soon as Maddy caught her breath, she ran over and picked up Fiana's wand.

Now the tables had been truly turned.

Both vampires glared down at her with such hatred that she flinched. She couldn't quite muster the courage to brandish the wand triumphantly. They were still deadly enough in their own right. Best not provoke them. Instead, she ran over to Moody and helped him to his feet.

"I've got Fiana's wand," she whispered as she urged him towards the limited shelter of the cliff face.

"However did you manage that, my dear?" he wheezed, not having fully recovered his own breath.

"My stone knocked it from her hand."

"Well done, my dear, well done indeed! Very impressive!"

Maddy waved up to her friends to let them know they were all right and gestured that they wanted to come back up.

Before Rowan could oblige, a gunshot cracked and stone splinters rained down on Maddy and Moody.

James hung over the balcony now aiming for Maddy.

"Really? A gun? A vampire with a gun. Are you serious?" Maddy said as she and Moody crouched and stumbled over corpses running towards the safety of the main doors.

A second shot flew over their heads. Before a third could be fired, they ducked inside.

A bolt of magic struck James's hand, disarming him. He watched Rowan disappear from sight above, and when he turned around to regroup with Fiana, he saw her holding Rex a foot off the ground by the throat.

"This is not a good day!" she spat through clenched teeth.

"You're choking me," Rex managed, grasping at her hands.

"Stop it!" Trudy cried. "Stop it! You're hurting him." She got to her knees and tried to reach Fiana and Rex, but with a lazy wave of her free hand, Fiana threw Trudy against the stone wall.

"My will! You fools! My will shall be done! It doesn't end this way!"

"Please, angel," Rex squeaked. His face was turning purple. "Please. I love you."

"You pathetic worthless piece of trash. Can't you see this isn't the time for sentimentality?" She threw him with all her force against the opposite wall.

Rex's head left a spot of blood smeared where it had hit. "Please," he said, caressing his throat. "I'll serve you. Always. You have my loyalty, sweet angel."

"Go get my wand, boy." She crossed her arms and waiting for him to stand, but he was so hurt that it took him too long for her tastes. In the blink of an eye, she was upon him again. Lifting him again by the throat, she carried him out to the balcony. "I said, fetch my wand, you mongrel."

"Stop!" Rowan's voice spoke from above.

"Or what, my love? Strike me, and the boy dies. Give up your wand now, or I will drop him."

"Never. You will not take this from me again."

"No!" Trudy crawled towards the balcony, blood dripped down her face and mixed with her tears.

"Step back, wizard," Fiana warned Rowan again. "Do you think I'm bluffing? What is this boy to me? He's nothing. Pathetic, worthless sheep. He's nothing to me, so go ahead, strike me down, lover. Let the boy fall to his death."

James rejoined Fiana on the balcony, and she gave him a knowing look.

"I'm giving my wand to a human," Rowan said, handing his wand to someone out of sight. "She can't use it, please let the boy and his mother go."

"Nothing? I'm nothing to you," Rex choked, holding tightly onto Fiana's arm. "I believed in you. I gave my soul to you."

"Yes." The coldness in her voice even chilled James. In a fluid blur of movement, she ripped the dagger from James's chest and thrust it into Rex's gut. "Error in judgment, methinks."

And with that, she did exactly as Rowan asked. Watching the sweet betrayal cross Rex's face, she let him go.

Desiccated corpses littered the inside of the Grand Chamber, motionless.

"Ew-wa!"

Maddy found their presence rather disturbing.

Her flashlight illuminated their path as she and Moody stepped over the dead, making their way towards the throne room.

Just before reaching it, Trudy screeched rushing past them towards the stairs. She was clenching her stomach and blood dripped from her head. "My son! My son!."

"What's happened?" Maddy said, stopping her.

"My son! She's killed Rex! Oh, sweet Jesus! She's killed my boy!" Tears streamed down her face and her shrill voice echoed through the empty chamber.

"Oh, my god." Maddy covered her mouth.

"I've got to get to him. Oh, dear God! Let him be okay. Please let him be okay!" Trudy continued down stairs, stumbling over the dead.

"He's still alive," Rowan said, emerging from the throne room. "I watched her let go, but I couldn't get to my wand fast enough to do much. I slowed his fall at the last moment, but it was too late. It all happed so fast. He is not well, but he is alive."

"Fiana?" Marlin asked.

"Of course. I disarmed James, and Fiana was in a rage. They got away. One moment they were there, and the next they were gone."

Ms. MacFey ran both hands through her chestnut hair then down her face, wiping her tears away and forcing calm.

Ralph patted her on the shoulder for comfort, but his face held a very grim expression. "Getting Rex to a hospital should be our next step."

"What would happen if I broke this?" Maddy held up Fiana's wand. "Would that stop her from hurting us again?"

"Is that?" Aidan asked, eyes wide.

"It sure is. Real cool, huh?"

"What?" April asked through her own silent tears. "What is everyone talking about? What's happening?"

"Maddy's got Fiana's wand." Aidan said.

"Really? How did you do that?"

"It sort of fell into my hands, so to speak. So, can I break it? I really, really feel like breaking something."

"Destroying it would probably be a bad idea," Rowan said. "True, much of her power is contained within it, but if you break it, she would just fashion and claim another one. However, if you hold it safe, she will be unable to make another. As long as you keep it from her, she will lack a great part of her magical powers. That is our best hope, but it is also very dangerous. There is no denying what she's capable of. Destruction and murder without remorse. She is no longer my wife."

Maddy nodded her understanding. There would be no casting the ring into the cracks of doom. No easy retribution. "Still, it's good I have it, right? This is an overwhelming advantage, right? I mean, we might actually get out alive."

"It's our best chance to hunt her down and destroy her. Let's do it now," Aidan declared.

"She's gone," Rowan said. "Let us tend to Rex and make him as comfortable as we can."

Trudy held Rex's limp body in her arms, hysterical. His blood covered her clothes and arms and hair. One hand was pressed firmly over the stab wound. Blood bubbled up around her hand.

"Please help me," she cried as the other's approached. "Do something. I know you can do something! Please help me!"

Moody and Rowan knelt on either side of Rex. "His wounds are extensive, Trudy," Moody said. "We have to get him to a hospital. I wish I could just wave my wand and make it all okay, but his injuries are too great for that."

Trudy let out a gutteral wail, like her very soul was being ripped apart.

"We can ease his pain," Rowan said.

"Call 911," Max said to Ralph. "Get someone to meet us in town."

Ralph stepped away and did just that.

Max knelt behind Trudy and supported her head and back. All the kids stood back against the cliff face, silent. They didn't know what to say, so they said nothing.

"Can you stabilize him until we can get him into town?" Max asked Rowan.

"I can ease his pain," Rowan repeated.

"And I can slow the bleeding." Moody's face drooped in sorrow at this turn of events. Grief filled his eyes.

Grief filled all their hearts watching Trudy holding her dying son in her arms, helpless. Weeping. Wailing.

Rowan and Moody did what magic they could. Rowan cast a spell around Rex's throat that made his neck immobile to prevent any further injury then lifted him out of Trudy's arms and carried him back to the van. Moody and Max held up Trudy between them. She could barely walk.

"Will he be all right?" she asked over and over and over again between sobs.

Each time, Max would say, "Everything is going to be okay."

Above them, stars filling the night sky twinkled and a beautiful full moon lit their way. The roar of a twin engine plane taking off nearby caused Maddy to look up towards the sound.

"I suppose that's our vampire couple on their way to cause more trouble for us from some other secret lair filled with who knows what kind of minions, probably werewolves with our luck."

Moody shrugged. "That has been her mode of operation up until now."

The walk back to the van took a long time and most of their remaining energy.

By the time they got to the van, they were exhausted. The adrenaline which had sustained them throughout the raid had drained away, leaving nothing but weariness behind.

The medevac helicopter from Reno met them in Gerlach. They said their goodbyes and wished Trudy well.

There was nothing more they could do, and Trudy didn't want any more of their help anyway. She had been quite clear about that on the ride to town.

"Now what do we do?" wondered Aidan, watching the helicopter take off.

Ralph responded, "We get home as soon as possible, before Fiana has time to hide her energy signature again. This isn't over."

CHAPTER TWENTY-SEVEN

Everyone silently consented and climbed into the van.

Maddy anticipated an excruciatingly long ride home. She sat between Rowan and April, but just as she started to doze on Rowan's strong shoulder, he was suddenly much shorter.

Rowan was no longer there.

"What are you doing here?"

Cullen gave her a wary look. "Believe me, I'm no happier about your presence, but it feels good to be back again." Maddy gave him a big hug.

"Are you hugging my prom date?" April said, and then threw her arms around Cullen, too.

"Welcome back, Cullen," Aidan said. "I missed my little brother." She kissed the top of his head.

Ralph and Max smiled at each other, and then she turned to Cullen and said, "Rest now, my little knight. It's going to be a long drive home."

CHAPTER TWENTY-EIGHT

Despite their weariness, no one wanted to stay anywhere even remotely near Fiana's former fastness. The same state was too close. Ralph volunteered to drive as long as he could while everyone else slept in the crowded van.

By the time dawn broke, Ralph couldn't go any further. He woke up Max to take over, and they continued towards home. Everyone else remained asleep.

They reached Redding an hour after noon. Everyone was awake by then, so they all trooped into a truck stop for a bathroom break and a sandwich.

They all climbed back into the van and Ralph resumed driving. By nightfall, they were home.

Their first stop was Moody's house. Everyone but Max and Ralph got off there. April and Maddy would stay for a meeting and sleep over, returning to their respective homes the following day.

They all had gotten enough sleep on the trip to want to talk about their recent adventures and discuss what to do next.

"We should go after her immediately," Aidan declared. "There isn't any point in waiting around for her to hatch some new scheme. We have her at a disadvantage and should use that before she comes up with a counter measure, especially after what she did to Rex. We can't let her get away with that."

"I agree." Cullen felt good to be home and in his own body again, but even though he hated Rex for the cruelty he had shown Cullen throughout his life, he didn't want him to be hurt this badly, and by Fiana.

"We agree we need to stop her," said Maddy, "but we need to find her first."

"Ralph is on that," Aidan said. "We need to come up with a plan to initiate when he does."

"When will that be?"

"Tomorrow, I hope."

Moody cleared his throat. "If I might intervene. I think the first thing we should decide is what to do with Fiana's wand."

"I was going to hang on to it. I found it, after all."

"I don't think that is a very good idea, my dear. It will make you a target and leave it too exposed to recovery by her."

Maddy looked disappointed. "What would you suggest?"

"I have a safe in the house, so let's put it there. I'll conceal it with magic, but I don't think it will work against the wand's owner. Tomorrow, I can have a chat with Ralph, find out what kind of engineering magic he can work in that regard. She's powerful, and she will want to get back."

Just then, doorbell chimes echoed through the house. Everyone looked surprised. Although the daylight lingered on this late August day, the hour had passed seven.

"Who would call at this time?" Cullen wondered. "I'll go see who it is." He half expected it to be Trudy for some reason he couldn't explain. The others, also curious, watched him walk through the sitting room and into the foyer. Two men stood on the porch wearing identical suits and carrying identical briefcases.

They even stood in identical postures. The only way he could tell them apart was that one was dark skinned with a wide, flat face while the other was lighter with a sharp nose like a beak. Or maybe it was just the distortion of the peep hole.

He considered going and telling the others, but remembering that vampires could not enter uninvited decided to open the door and find out what they wanted. He disengaged the dead bolt, removed the security chain, and opened the door.

"Can I help you?"

The one with the flat face doffed his hat.

"I apologize for disturbing you this evening, but we are from the firm of Sirs Arthur and Duncan. We are looking for one Cullen Knight. Would he be in residence?"

"I'm Cullen Knight. What do you want?"

The second man with the beak-nose continued, "There is a certain matter of a legacy, bequeathed to you by your parents. We are intrusted in seeing to the fulfillment of certain requirements. May we come in?"

Cullen did not hesitate: "No."

The two lawyers looked at each other and nodded. They both displayed the barest hints of smiles.

"That is good," declared the first speaker. "We are here because inquiries—"

"—and generous donations—" the second one added.

"—have been made."

"Will you accept our card?" asked the second, holding forth a small white rectangle of paper. Cullen reached out a hand and accepted it, pulling it quickly to his side of the threshold. He looked at it. It had nothing written on it, but had turned a deep forest green. He looked up at his visitors in confusion. They were looking at each other and nodding. The second one turned to him.

"The requirements have been fulfilled. You are indeed Cullen Knight. The legacy is yours." The first lawyer squatted down and set his briefcase flat on the porch. With a snap, the locks sprang open. He removed a hand bound book with an ornate leather cover and handed it through the doorway to Cullen, who accepted it with great curiosity.

The man then closed his case and stood up.

The second man nodded to him. "Is there a Mr. Marlin in residence?"

"Yes. I will go get him. But I'm going to close the door in the meantime. Wait here."

Both men nodded their understanding, so Cullen closed the door, engaged the bolt, and slid the security chain back in its slot. He carried the book he'd been given carefully back to the room where the others waited for him.

"There are some lawyers at the door who want to talk to Uncle Marlin."

Moody looked surprised, but got out of his chair and went to see what they wanted.

Cullen sat down with the book on his lap.

"What's up?" Maddy asked.

Cullen looked at her numbly. "It's the legacy."

"What is?" asked Aidan.

Mutely, Cullen raised the book from his lap. "I wasn't supposed to get this until I graduated from high school. The Samuels always thought it was money, but this is so much cooler!"

"Yeah. Way cool!" declared Maddy. "That looks really old. Is that what Moody was after?"

"I guess so."

"Well, what's in it?"

Cullen shrugged. He opened the book and flipped through the pages. "Weird. It's just full of these funny spirals. I can't make sense of it."

"I can," said Rowan within his head. "Remember the runes carved on the tree where you found my wand? It is the same script."

Just then, Moody came back into the room holding a thick envelope. "In here lies the answer."

na deireadh

ABOUT THE AUTHORS

Christine and Ethan Rose have marvelous imaginations. Often finding their inspiration among the trees, they write as they lead their lives—with plenty of adventure, magic, and love. They met swing dancing in 1999 and were married a year later. Throughout 2009-2011, they toured the U.S. in a fancifully painted RV, affectionately called the Geekalicous Gypsy Caravan, to promote their first book *Rowan of the Wood*. Sadly, they had to part with the GGC in 2012.

Although many tragic heroes begin as orphans, Ethan actually was one. Living in foster care in Sonoma County, he grew up amongst the magical redwoods in Northern California and continues to read every fantasy novel he can get his hands on. Anglophile Christine holds her M.A. in Medieval/Renaissance Literature & Folklore and wrote her Master's Thesis on *Le Morte D'arthur*. She is an entrepreneur at heart and is often described as a "free spirit."

Christine's scholarly, goal-oriented background mixed with Ethan's in-depth knowledge of modern fantasy creates an impenetrable team of writers who look forward to writing many more books together. When not at home in Austin, they can be found at various Celtic Festivals and Renaissance Faires around the country, their three canine kids and Shadow, the cat, in tow.

Power of the Zephyr is the fourth novel in their *Rowan of the Wood* five-book fantasy series.

Learn more about the authors at *www.ChristineAndEthanRose.com*
Official book site & other fun stuff *www.RowanOfTheWood.com*

OTHER TITLES FROM BLUE MOOSE PRESS

Rowan of the Wood
Winner of the 2009 Indie Excellence Award
978-0-9819949-2-5 $12.95 trade paperback
After a millennium of imprisonment in his magic wand, an ancient
wizard possesses the young boy who released him. When danger is
nigh, he emerges from the frightened child to set things right. Both
he and the boy try to grasp what has happened to them only to dis-
cover a deeper problem. Somehow the wizard's bride from the ancient
past has survived and become something evil.
http://www.rowanofthewood.com

Witch on the Water
Rowan of the Wood: Book Two
978-0-9819949-2-5 $12.95 trade paperback
Cullen thought he had enough trouble surviving school, dealing with
his miserable home life, and being possessed by Rowan, a 1400-year-
old wizard. But when Rowan's wife, the sadistic vampire Fiana,
comes back seeking revenge, Cullen and his band of misfits must
do what they can to stop her. This time Cullen's favorite teacher is
Fiana's first target.

Fire of the Fey
Rowan of the Wood: Book Three
978-0-9819949-6-3 $12,95 trade paperback
Adventures continue for Cullen Knight and his band of misfits in this
third installment of the Rowan of the Wood fantasy series. Still possessed by the wizard Rowan, Cullen settles into his new home with
his fire elemental sister, Aidan, and their fey uncle, Moody Marlin.
But all is not well. A series of fires raging through the redwoods puts
Aidan in the hot seat, as the group looks to her for an explanation.

Maddy's mother discovers a dark and disturbing secret, Ralph and
Max are off to a rocky start, and Rex adopts a holy crusade with a
mysterious angel as his guide.

Titles by O. M. Grey, Christine's Steampunk Alter Ego:

Avalon Revisited
978-0-9819949-5-6 $10.99 trade paperback
Arthur Tudor has made his existence as a vampire bearable for over three hundred years by immersing himself in blood and debauchery. Aboard an airship gala, he meets Avalon, an aspiring vampire slayer who sparks fire into Arthur's shriveled heart. Together they try to solve the mystery of several horrendous murders on the dark streets of London. Cultures clash and pressures rise in this sexy Steampunk Romance.
http://omgrey.wordpress.com

The Zombies of Mesmer
978-1-936960-92-7 $12.95 trade paperback
Gothic YA paranormal romance novel
Follow Nicole Knickerbocker Hawthorn (Nickie Nick) as she discovers her destiny as The Protector, a powerful vampire hunter. Ashe, a dark and mysterious stranger, helps Nickie and her friends solve the mystery behind several bizarre disappearances. Suitable for teens, enjoyed by adults.

Caught in the Cogs: An Eclectic Collection
978-1-936960-90-3 $12.95 trade paperback
In the midst of war, a beautiful young officer finds love aboard an airship...A woman steals away to fulfill her desire with a phantom lover...A group of thieves seek out a town of women to satisfy their lustful urges, but these ladies have an agenda of their own...

PLUS nine more short stories, angsty love poetry, and twenty-six relationship essays considering topics such as alternative lifestyles, deepening intimacy, opening communication, abusive relationships, and how to end a relationship with respect.

Prelude to a Change of Mind
Hidden Lands of Nod: Book One
978-0-9827426-0-0 $9.95 trade paperback
Meg Christmas is found sick unto death in a remote mountain camp. Beings out of legend arrive to save her, emerging from an alternate realm where they live in exile. A quiet, intimate adventure, *Prelude to a Change of Mind* boasts dire peril and brave feats, but also lots of tea with Ekaterina Rigidstick, poems by Jack Plenty, and talks with both about the nature of reality and conditions of being.

Entranscing
Hidden Lands of Nod: Book Two
978-0-9827426-2-4 $9.95 trade paperback
The second book in *The Hidden Lands of Nod* revisits Meg and her friends from the exile realms of the Dvarsh—the metamath-emage, Ekaterina Rigidstick, and her cousin, the part-human poet, Jackanapes Plenty—in a vastly different reality twenty years on. This fast-moving follow-on to *Prelude to a Change of Mind* picks up and enlarges the tale of Meg, the Dvarsh, the Thrm, and their collective struggle to save both love and the planet.
http://www.robertstikmanz.com

Fiends: Volume One
978-1-936960-00-2 $35.00 Limited Edition Hardback
978-1-936960-01-9 $12.95 trade paperback
Including Canvas, Tattoo, and Closet Treats, Fiends: Vol 1 is a collection of horror stories by Paul E. Cooley. As a special treat, the author gives his reader a glimpse into the FiendMaster's Scrapbook.

All Blue Moose Press titles are also available in Kindle and other eReader versions. For more information on our current titles, as well as other exciting titles on the horizon, visit
http://thebluemoosepress.com

GET AUTHOR SIGNED BOOKS DIRECT FROM
THE PUBLISHER and SUPPORT INDIE AUTHORS!